SUE GRAFTON

"L" is for Lawless

Retold by John Escott

MACMILLAN

MACMILLAN READERS

ELEMENTARY LEVEL

Founding Editor: John Milne

The Macmillan Readers provide a choice of enjoyable reading materials for learners of English. The series is published at six levels – Starter, Beginner, Elementary, Pre-intermediate, Intermediate and Upper.

Level control

Information, structure and vocabulary are controlled to suit the students' ability at each level.

The number of words at each level:

Starter	about 300 basic words
Beginner	about 600 basic words
Elementary	about 1100 basic words
Pre-intermediate	about 1400 basic words
Intermediate	about 1600 basic words
Upper	about 2200 basic words

Vocabulary

Some difficult words and phrases in this book are important for understanding the story. Some of these words are explained in the story and some are shown in the pictures. From Pre-intermediate level upwards, words are marked with a number like this: ...³. These words are explained in the Glossary at the end of the book.

Answer keys

Answer keys for the *Points for Understanding* can be found at www.macmillanenglish.com

Contents

Notes About the Author and This Story

Sue Grafton was born on April 24th, 1940, in Louisville, Kentucky in the U.S.A. Her father, C.W. Grafton, was a writer of mystery stories. Before she became a novelist, Sue Grafton wrote scripts for TV plays. She lives with her husband in Santa Barbara, California.

"A" is for Alibi was Sue Grafton's first crime detection novel. The main character of the story is Kinsey Millhone, a thirty-five-year-old female private investigator—a private detective. Kinsey does not work for the police. People hire her—they pay her—to find out the truth. Each of her jobs is called a case. Sometimes she has to investigate crimes. The crime may be a murder, or a robbery. Sometimes she has to find things that are lost or people who are missing. When she has finished her investigation, Kinsey writes a report.

After "A" is for Alibi, Sue Grafton wrote "B" is for Burglar[1], then fifteen other stories about Kinsey Millhone. "Q" is for Quarry was published in 2003. The author is going to write twenty-six stories about Kinsey's cases, one for each letter of the alphabet.

In this story, Kinsey lives and works in Santa Teresa, a town in the state of California. Santa Teresa is not a real town, but most of the other places that Kinsey visits are real. In "L" is for Lawless, Kinsey travels to the states of Arkansas (pronounced: **arkansaw**), Texas and Kentucky.

The Places in This Story

5

The People in This Story

Kinsey Millhone

Henry Pitts

William Pitts

Johnny Lee

Ray Rawson

Rosie

Chester Lee

Bucky Lee

Babe Lee

Gilbert Hays

Laura Huckaby

Helen Rawson

1

A Favor[2] for Henry

In the future, I'll hesitate[3] before I do a favor for the friend of a friend. I nearly died. *And* I didn't get paid.

Before I explain what happened, here are a few personal facts. My name is Kinsey Millhone, I'm thirty-five, and I'm a private investigator. I live and work in the town of Santa Teresa, in southern California. I've been married twice and divorced[4] twice. I have no children. Before I became a private detective, I worked in the Santa Teresa Police Department. I live alone in a small apartment that had once been a garage. The apartment belongs to my landlord[5], Henry Pitts.

The Lawless case started with a request from my landlord, Henry Pitts. Everybody knows that I love Henry like a father. He's eighty-five and he would do anything for me. And it's not often that he asks *me* for anything, so I couldn't refuse to help him.

It was Thursday, November 21st, the week before Thanksgiving[6]. Henry's older brother, William, was going to marry my friend, Rosie, on Thanksgiving Day. They were going to have their wedding at the restaurant that Rosie owns. Rosie is seventy and William is nearly eighty-eight.

I was taking a week's vacation because of Rosie and William's wedding. I was going help Henry with the wedding preparations. There were going to be eight guests at the wedding: Rosie's sister, Klotilde, Henry and his brothers, Lewis and Charlie, and their sister Nell. And me.

Henry calls his brothers "the boys" but he is the youngest in his family. Charlie is ninety-three, Lewis is eighty-nine, and Nell is ninety-five.

I saw Henry at nine o'clock that Thursday morning. I

opened the door of my apartment and he was standing outside.

"I was going to leave you a note," Henry said. "I'm on my way to the airport. I'm going to pick up Nell and the boys. But I wanted to ask if you'll do me a favor."

"What's the favor?" I said. "I was going to the market, but I can go later."

"Do you remember old Johnny Lee? He lived around the corner, on Bay Street. He had a little white house—a cottage—although he didn't live in it himself. Johnny lived in an apartment above the garage. Johnny's grandson Bucky and his wife have been living in the house."

"I pass the house when I go running in the morning," I said, "but I don't know Mr Lee or his family."

"You've probably seen the Lees at Rosie's restaurant," Henry said. "Bucky's wife is called Babe and she's short and fat. Johnny's clothes were old and untidy and he looked like a homeless person, but he had a home and a little money."

I was beginning to remember the Lee family. "You used the past tense," I said. "Is the old man dead?"

"Yes. Johnny died sometime in July," Henry said. "He was only in his seventies, but he must have had a weak heart. He died from a heart attack. I think that he was a fighter pilot[7] during World War Two. He was a member of the American Volunteer Group. Sometimes he talked about Burma[8] and the air battles over Rangoon."

"So what's the problem?"

"When Johnny Lee died he was cremated[9]," Henry said. "Johnny had fought during the war. So Bucky thought that maybe his grandfather could have a military burial. He also thought that the government would pay for the funeral. Bucky talked to his father, Chester, about it and Chester thought that it was a good idea. So Bucky filled out[10] the official forms, and sent them off to the Veterans

Administration Office[11]. He didn't have *all* the information about his grandfather but he did what he could. More than three months passed, then the papers came back marked 'Cannot identify.'

"Bucky called his Dad and told him the news," Henry went on. "Chester Lee phoned Randolph Air Force Base in Texas, where the Air Force keeps its personnel files[12]. But the Air Force has no record of John Lee. Or if they do know about him, they won't talk to his family. Chester is angry, and he's determined[13] to get a military burial for Johnny. I thought that maybe you could help."

"I'll talk to Bucky, if you want me to," I said.

"And Chester is visiting here from Columbus, Ohio," Henry said. "I know that they would be glad to have your help. You could tell them what to do next."

———

The Lees' cottage had an old red roof, and the white walls needed painting. There was a two-car garage at the end of a narrow driveway. A Ford car that was broken into several pieces was lying in the yard. I had to walk through shoulder-high grass to get to the front door. I rang the door bell and waited. The door was opened moments later by a guy who I recognized. Bucky was in his early twenties, and he had long red hair and an untidy beard. He wore a blue shirt that was hanging out at the back of his jeans.

"Are you Bucky Lee?" I asked.

Bucky looked at me for a few moments before he replied.

"Yeah," he said in a slow, dull voice.

I held out my hand. "I'm Kinsey Millhone—a friend of Henry Pitts."

"You're the private detective?" he said.

"You've probably seen me at Rosie's restaurant," I said.

"Sure, I remember," he said at last. "I often eat there. Come in." He stepped back and I moved into a small hallway[14]. "My dad isn't here right now," he said, "and I think that Babe is in the shower." He turned and shouted loudly, "Hey, *Babe*!" Then he turned back toward me. "Have a seat. I'll go and find her."

I went into the untidy living room and sat down. There were bookcases with tall piles of papers and magazines on them. A small table was covered with dirty plates.

Bucky returned. "Babe will be here in a minute. We've got to go somewhere soon and she's getting dressed. My dad will be back in about two hours."

"How long have you lived here?" I asked.

"Nearly two years—since Babe and I got married."

"I used to see your grandfather at Rosie's," I said. "But I don't think that we ever met."

"That's Pappy—my grandfather—over there," Bucky said. He nodded toward a shelf over the fireplace. There was a metal box on it.

"Babe and me paid $300 to have him cremated and we'd like our money back," Bucky said. "I guess the government will pay another $150 for Pappy's burial. It's not much, I know, but we don't have a lot of money. We can't pay you. Did Henry tell you?"

"It's OK. There's not much that I can do anyway."

Bucky gave me some papers—John Lee's death certificate[15], his birth certificate, his social security card[16], and copies of the forms requesting the burial money and John Lee's military records.

I looked at the documents. "There's a lot of information missing," I said. "Don't you know your grandfather's Air Force number, or the unit[17] that he served[18] in?"

"No."

"Did Johnny receive a military pension[19]?"

"If he did, he never told us," Bucky said. "Pappy got his social security checks, and Dad gave him some money too.

10

Pappy didn't like banks. He kept his money in a coffee jar behind the refrigerator. Babe and me paid him rent[20] of $600 a month. He lived in the apartment above the garage. It's just a couple of little rooms, but they're nice. And now there's a guy who wants to rent the apartment."

I read the form that requested Johnny's military records.

"When did your grandfather leave the Air Force?" I asked. "You didn't write that down."

"Oh, I forgot to fill out that part of the form," Bucky said. "Dad says that Pappy came home on August 17th, 1944. Dad remembers that because it was just before his fourth birthday party. Pappy was away fighting for two years. So he must have left home and joined the Air Force sometime in 1942."

"Did your grandfather keep any old letters from his Air Force days? Did he keep any old photographs?"

"We didn't find anything like that yet," he said. "Do you want to come and look?"

I followed Bucky out of the cottage and across the driveway to the garage. We climbed the wooden stairs to the door of Johnny Lee's apartment. While Bucky looked for the door key, I looked through the window. I could see two rooms but there was no door between them. There was only a door frame.

I followed Bucky into the apartment. The air inside smelled of cigarette smoke. The main room had a narrow bed and some old furniture. There was a small wooden desk and chair in one corner, and ten or twelve cardboard boxes on the floor. Some of the boxes were filled with Johnny's things.

I went through the door frame to the kitchen. Beyond the kitchen, there was a very small bathroom. Bucky had said that the apartment was nice. But I'd rather shoot myself than finish my life in a place like it.

I looked out of one of the windows. Bucky's wife, Babe, was standing outside the back door of the cottage. She had a round face with big brown eyes, and dark hair.

"Bucky!" she called.

"I'm coming!" he shouted. Then he said to me, "Is it OK if I just leave you here?" He gave me the key. "Lock the door when you've finished. If you find anything that looks important, tell us later. We'll be back at about one o'clock."

I watched Bucky and Babe lock the door of the cottage and then open the garage door beneath me. An old green car came out a few moments later, and they drove away. I should have left then. But I remembered Henry's request. I should at least *pretend*[21] to search for some clues.

I spent the next few minutes searching the rooms of Johnny Lee's apartment. The bathroom and kitchen contained nothing important. I checked[22] the pockets of Johnny's clothes in the bedroom closet[23]. I found no clues there. I sat down at his small desk and began opening the drawers. Bucky had removed most of the old man's papers. There were no bills[24], old checks, or letters from a bank. I got up and looked in some of the cardboard boxes. In one box I found a lot of books about World War Two.

———

I was looking through Johnny's books when I heard someone coming up the wooden stairs. I went to the door. A man in his sixties, with thinning[25] white hair, was outside.

"Is Bucky up here?" he asked.

"No, he'll be back at about one o'clock. Are you Chester?"

"No." He smiled. "My name is Ray Rawson. I'm—I *was* an old friend of Johnny's." The man wore cotton trousers, a clean white T-shirt and tennis shoes.

"I'm Kinsey Millhone—a neighbor," I said.

"Are you hoping to rent the apartment?"

"Oh, no," I said. "Are you?"

"Well, I hope to. But Bucky and his dad keep getting new ideas. First, Bucky and his wife decided to live in the apartment and rent out the cottage instead. Then, Chester

"My name is Ray Rawson."

said that he wanted the apartment for when he comes to visit. I was hoping to move in here sometime this week. I offered to help them to get all of Johnny's things out. I've come from Ashland, Kentucky and I've been staying in a hotel. Anyway, it's not your problem. I'm sorry that I stopped you working."

"It's OK," I said. "I'm just looking through some boxes."

Ray Rawson entered the room and watched me. "Are you searching for something?"

"Yes, I'm hoping to find some information about Johnny's military service. Did you serve in the Air Force with him?"

"No," he said. "We both worked at Jefferson Boat Works outside Louisville, Kentucky. That was just after the war started. I was twenty, Johnny was ten years older. He was a clever guy, he taught me a lot. Can I help you?"

I shook my head. "No, thanks. I've almost finished. How well did you know Johnny?" I started putting the books back into the boxes.

"We phoned or wrote to each other once or twice a year. I knew that he had a family here in California, but I never met them until now." He began to help me with the books. "I've been living in Ashland, but Johnny always told me to visit him if I came to California. Well, a few months ago I decided to come here. I didn't know that Johnny was dead."

"How long have you been in Santa Teresa?" I asked.

"A little more than a week," he said. "I didn't plan to stay, but I like California, it's nice. I want to rent Johnny's apartment. I hope that Bucky doesn't think that this is a strange idea. Johnny wouldn't mind if I lived here, I'm sure."

"Where are you staying now?"

"At the Lexington Hotel, near the beach."

"Well, I think I'll stop searching," I said.

Ray left the apartment ahead of me and waited while I locked the door. I followed him down the stairs and I put the key through the mail slot[26] in the front door of the cottage.

14

"Thanks for your help," I said to Ray.

He lifted one hand, gave a quick wave, and walked off.

When I got home, the door of Henry's house was open and I could hear voices in his kitchen. Nell, Charlie and Lewis had arrived.

A few minutes later, I drove to the supermarket. Afterwards, I went to the bank and got fifty dollars in cash. Then I filled my car with gas and came home again. I was putting my food away in the refrigerator when the phone rang. It was Bucky.

"Hi, Kinsey," he said. "Come over here to Bay Street, will you? Somebody broke into Pappy's apartment."

2

Johnny Lee

When I reached the Lees' house, Babe opened the front door.

"Hi, I'm Kinsey," I said. "Bucky called me."

"Oh, yeah," she said. "Nice to meet you." She stepped back to let me enter and I followed her through the hallway to the living room. "Chester has been shouting about the break-in ever since we got home."

"Did Bucky and Chester call the police?" I asked.

"Yeah, they're on their way."

"And you just got home?"

"Bucky and me got home a little while ago," Babe said. "Chester got home first. He'd bought a new light and went to fix it in the apartment. He saw the broken window and all the glass on the steps. Somebody made a real[27] mess."

"Did the burglar take anything?"

"We're trying to find out. Chester told Bucky that he was wrong to leave you alone in the apartment this morning."

"Me?" I said. "Why would I break in and make the place untidy?"

"That's what Bucky said, but Chester never listens to him."

I followed Babe up the stairs to the garage apartment. The door was open and there was a hole in the window next to it. Someone had broken the glass. Then the person had put their hand inside the window, and unlocked the door.

Chester heard us and came out of the apartment. He was a big man with blond hair down to his shoulders. He had small blue eyes and a red face. He wore a gold earring in one ear and his blue shirt was hanging outside his jeans.

I held my hand out. "Kinsey Millhone, Mr Lee. I understand that you're upset."

"You can drop the 'Mr Lee'," he said. "Just call me Chester." He shook my hand. "Yeah, I'm upset. I don't know what Bucky asked you to do, but it wasn't this."

I looked past him into the apartment. Books, bedsheets, pillows and clothes were lying on the floor. I could see that all the pots and pans were thrown across the kitchen floor. But none of these things were damaged or destroyed.

Bucky came out of the kitchen. "The toilet is broken," he said. "But maybe it was broken before this happened."

Chester pointed a finger at him. "You'll pay for it. It was your idea to ask her to come here," he said angrily.

He turned to me. "It's a real mess in there…" He went on and on about the things that were broken. He was one of those guys who enjoy complaining.

I began to get angry. "Hey, I didn't do this, Chester. The place was OK when I left. Ray Rawson was here, ask him."

"Are you saying that Ray Rawson did this?" he said.

"No, of course not! Why would Ray Rawson break in?

16

"Hey, I didn't do this, Chester. The place was OK when I left."

He's hoping to move in here himself."

"Well, talk to him and find out what he knows."

"What could he know? He left at the same time as me."

"I'm going downstairs to wait for the police," Chester said. "Bucky, you and Babe can clean the place up."

"This is a crime scene[28]," I said. "Don't touch anything. The police might want to look for fingerprints."

Chester's face seemed to become a darker red. "There's something not right about this," he said angrily and looked at me. "Come with me."

On the way down the stairs I glanced[29] at my watch. It was 1:15 p.m.

————

Chester went into the kitchen of Bucky's cottage and started to make some sandwiches. As he did this, he slowly became calmer and his anger disappeared.

"I'm sorry that I was angry with you," he said at last, "but I don't like what's going on here. I sent Bucky to live with his grandfather, but it was a mistake. I thought that they could look after each other. The next thing I hear is that Bucky has married that girl, Babe. She's all right—she's stupid, but so is Bucky. I just don't think that they should be married. Pappy probably encouraged Babe and Bucky to get married. My dad liked to make trouble."

Chester made sandwiches for both of us and we sat and ate them. I wanted to know more about him.

"What work do you do in Columbus?" I asked.

"I have a small shop in Bexley," he explained. "I print brochures, office stationery, business cards. But it's time that I did something else. I'm too young to retire[30], but I'm tired of working."

"Do you want to leave Ohio and come to live here, in California?"

"I don't know," Chester replied. "Pappy came to Santa

Teresa in 1945 and bought this place. I grew up here, but I left it when I was eighteen."

"Johnny died after a heart attack?" I said.

"Yeah. It happened one Saturday night. He'd eaten his supper here and he stood up to go back to his apartment. He fell and died before he got to the stairs."

"And now somebody has broken into Johnny's apartment," I said. "Do you think that this is connected[31] with his death?"

"Maybe there is a connection," he said. "But I don't believe that he was murdered." He hesitated for a second, then went on speaking. "You have to understand something about my father. Pappy had secrets. He didn't like to talk about some things, especially the war. He would never answer questions about it, or what he did then."

"Why?"

"Think about this for a moment," Chester said. "Pappy dies and Bucky gets the idea of asking for money to give Pappy a military burial." He looked at me carefully. "Bucky contacts the VAO and fills out a form. And that's when someone from the government comes here."

"Someone from the government?" I repeated.

He moved closer and spoke quietly. "I think that my dad was hiding from the FBI[32]."

I stared at him. "Why would Johnny be hiding from the Federal Bureau of Investigation?"

"Listen, in all the years since the war Pappy never asked for anything from the government. He didn't ask for a war veteran's pension—nothing. Why not?"

"Surprise me," I said.

He smiled. "All right, make a joke of it, but look at the facts. We fill out a form and the VAO says that they have no record of him. What do they mean? The VAO must have Pappy's personnel files. All servicemen's records are kept by the government. So I phone the Randolph Air Force Base in Texas. They say: 'We have no war record for a fighter pilot named John Lee.' Next I call the National Personnel Records Center in St Louis. 'Not known,' they say. Finally, I call the Pentagon[33] in Virginia. Nothing. Everyone says, 'No records.'"

Chester pointed a finger toward the garage apartment.

"Then someone breaks into Pappy's apartment. Do you understand what I'm saying?"

"No, I don't."

"I think that the FBI sent someone here to look through the things in Pappy's apartment," he said. "I think that Pappy was a double agent[34] during World War Two."

"Oh, stop this! You're saying that your father was a…a *spy*?"

"A kind of spy, yes. I think that the government is pretending that they don't have his records," Chester said.

I stared at him. "Are you saying that he worked for our enemies, or spied on them for our people?"

"I think that maybe he worked for the Japanese, but I can't be sure. The U.S. fought the Japanese in World War Two. A few times, Pappy talked about the air battles between the Japanese and the U.S. air forces over Rangoon in Burma."

"Do you think that Johnny *was* in the U.S. Air Force?" I asked.

"Why would he lie about a thing like that?" Chester replied.

"OK, so let's pretend that he *was* a spy during the Second World War," I said. "That was more than forty years ago. Johnny is *dead* now, so why does anybody care?"

"Maybe he took something from someone and they want it back. Maybe he took secret files or documents. I don't know. But did these people find what they were looking for, or is it still hidden somewhere? Maybe this Rawson guy is connected with the break-in."

I put my hands on my head. This was crazy. "Well, it's an interesting idea but investigating government spies is not my kind of work," I said. "Thanks for the sandwich."

There was a sudden knock at the back door and I jumped round.

Chester stood up. "That must be the police," he said. "Don't say anything to them about this."

He went to the front door and returned to the kitchen with a police officer.

"Thank you for coming, officer. This is my neighbor, Kinsey Millhone," Chester said in pleasant, friendly voice.

"Do you want me to stay?" I asked Chester.

"It's OK, I'll call you later," he said.

———

I went to Henry's house for dinner that evening. Henry's three brothers and his sister were there. Rosie came too, and as soon as she and William saw each other they couldn't stop smiling.

It was Lewis's eighty-ninth birthday, so we sang "Happy Birthday" to him.

After dinner, Henry took me to a quiet part of the room and asked me about the break-in at Johnny Lee's apartment.

"Chester thinks that the break-in is connected to his dad's death," I told him. "He thinks that Johnny was a double agent during World War Two and that he had some stolen documents. Chester thinks that government agents broke in to the apartment to look for the documents. *I* think that he's seen too many bad movies."

"Chester is crazy," Henry said. "Well, you did what you could. Thanks, Kinsey."

3

The Key

The next morning I went for a run. I do this every day. It's the only healthy thing that I do. I don't eat healthy food, I don't often take vacations, and I don't get enough rest. It was one of those perfect November days in California. The sun was just rising in the sky and the air was cool. There was a smell of smoke from wood fires.

When I got home, I had a shower. As I was finishing my breakfast, the phone rang. I glanced at the clock. The time was 7:41 a.m.

"Hello?" I said.

"It's me, Chester," the voice said. "I've got something that I want to show you. We found it last night."

"What kind of 'it'?" I asked.

"Just come over here and I'll show you. Bucky found it when he was cleaning Pappy's place." Chester sounded pleased with himself.

When I got to Bucky's cottage, I went immediately to the garage apartment. The door was open and I could hear voices. Inside, Bucky and Chester were standing near the empty clothes closet. Babe was putting Johnny's clothes into an old suitcase.

Chester smiled when he saw me. "Come over here and look at this," he said.

Bucky stepped to the side and showed me a wooden panel[35] that he'd pulled away from the back of the closet. In the hole behind the panel, there was a small safe[36].

"How did you find that?" I asked.

"I was cleaning the closet," Bucky said. "I knocked my brush against the back of the closet and it sounded strange.

So I pushed the back of the closet again, and this panel opened."

"A locksmith[37] is coming," Chester told me.

"Have you looked for the combination to the safe?" I asked. "Maybe Johnny wrote down the number and put it somewhere."

"We looked in every place that we could think of. What about you? When you were here yesterday, did you find a list of numbers that could be a combination?"

"I never saw a list of numbers," I said. "But maybe Johnny used his birth date or his social security number."

Bucky and Chester slowly lifted the heavy metal safe out of the space at the back of the closet and put it on the floor. Then we waited. Before an hour had passed, the locksmith arrived. The four of us watched as he worked. He cut holes in the lock using special tools. At last he pulled the handle and the door opened.

Babe said, "It's empty!"

"So they got it already," Chester said, angrily.

"Got what?" Babe asked, but Chester didn't answer.

While the locksmith put his tools into his bag, Bucky bent down and shone a flashlight inside the safe. "There's something in here, Dad," he said.

Chester and I knelt on the floor and looked inside the safe too. There was a piece of adhesive tape[38] holding something inside the top of the safe. "What's that?" Chester said. "Let me look at that thing."

Bucky carefully removed the tape. A big iron key was attached to it. He held it up. "Does anybody recognize this?" he asked.

"No, but Pappy liked to play with locks," Chester said. "He worked for a locksmith back in the 1930s."

I turned the key over in my hand. It was old and quite beautiful really.

I turned the key over in my hand.

I showed the key to the locksmith. "Do you have any ideas about this?" I asked.

"It looks like a key for a big gate," he replied. Then he closed his tool bag and Chester took him down to the cottage to pay him.

"Now what do we do?" Bucky asked.

"I have a friend who knows a lot about locks," I said. "Maybe he can tell us about the kind of lock that this key might fit. Shall I ask him?"

"That's OK with me," Bucky said.

I put the key in my pocket. I didn't tell them that my "friend" was a burglar.

As soon as I got home, I sat down at my desk and started making notes on small cards. When I'd written down all the facts that I could remember, I pinned all the cards on the wall above my desk. Then I sat back in my chair and studied them. Something wasn't right. I tried to remember something that I'd read about Burma. I also tried to remember something that I'd heard about the American Volunteer Group.

Which Air Force unit did Johnny serve in? When I'd looked through his books, I'd seen the names of several AVG fighter pilots. Some of those guys would be alive today. Maybe they could tell me.

I called my burglar friend, but he didn't seem to be at that phone number any more. Later I would contact the Santa Teresa Police Department. The police probably knew where he was.

———

By 10 a.m. I was at Bucky's, knocking on the cottage door. Nobody answered and the car wasn't in the garage. Maybe the three of them had gone out to breakfast.

There was a large pile of cardboard boxes and old furniture in the garage. The box, which was full of World War Two books, was on the top of the pile. I pulled the box over to the stairs, sat down, and started looking at the books. After a minute or two, I found what I was looking for—a book called *Fighter! The Story of Air Combat from 1936 to 1945* by Robert Jackson. I started to read.

On July 4th, 1942, the American Volunteer Group became part of the China Task Force. Almost all the AVG pilots who served in Burma later went to different parts of the world. A few remained in China and became part of the 23rd Fighter Group.

Johnny was overseas for two years. He came home in time for Chester's fourth birthday party on August 17th, 1944. But the AVG became part of the China Task Force two years before that date. Had Johnny served with the AVG or not? Had he ever fought *at all*? Was that why he didn't talk much about the war?

Well, the old guy was dead. His son and grandson believed that he was a war hero (or a spy) and that made them happy. I wasn't being paid to prove[39] that Johnny told lies about his war service. I wasn't being paid to do anything. In fact, I wasn't being *paid*. But I have to know the truth about things. Sometimes I get hurt, but I'll always try to find out the truth.

I looked at the big iron key again. There was a name written on it. Was it the name of the company who had made its lock? I couldn't read the letters easily, so I put the key back in my pocket.

I decided to go and see Ray Rawson. He had worked with Johnny sometime in 1942, after the war started. But why had he suddenly decided to come and see Johnny? Was there a special reason?

The Lexington Hotel was on a narrow street near the beach. It was a tired-looking building with a big crack down one wall. There wasn't a clerk at the reception desk in the lobby[40], so I picked up the phone on the desk and asked the operator[41] to connect me with Ray Rawson's room. The phone rang twice before Ray answered it. He told me to come up to his room—number 407.

The room had white walls and white drapes beside the windows. The view out of the windows was to the back of the building across the street.

"Has Bucky said anything about me renting the apartment?" Ray asked, smiling.

"He hasn't said anything to me," I said. "Did you hear that there was a break-in at Johnny's apartment?"

"When was this?"

I told Ray the story and watched his smile disappear.

"That's terrible," he said. "Wait a minute! You don't think that I had anything to do with the break-in, do you?"

"It's strange," I said. "Johnny died four months ago. There was no problem until you arrived in Santa Teresa. You got here last week and now Chester suddenly has problems."

"Listen, I wasn't in Bay Street last night. I was in the bar in this hotel. You can ask anyone."

"Can I sit down?" I asked.

"Yeah, of course," he said. We both sat down. "I'm probably the oldest and best friend that Johnny ever had," Ray went on. "I'd never do anything against Johnny. You've got to believe me."

"If I didn't believe you, I'd tell the police to look for your fingerprints at the apartment," I said.

"Didn't they do that?" he said.

"No. Chester didn't think that anything was missing. The person hadn't stolen anything. The police only look for fingerprints at the scene of a serious crime. For instance, when the crime is burglary." I watched Ray's face. "Is your home in Ashland?" I asked.

A second or two passed before Ray answered my question.

27

"I've got family there," he said.

"Did Johnny really serve in the Air Force?"

"I don't know," he replied. "I told you, I didn't hear from him for years."

"How did he find you after the war?"

Ray started to get annoyed. "Johnny had my address. What do you think that I've done? I don't have to answer all these questions."

"Chester thinks that Johnny was a spy during the war," I said. "He thinks that Johnny was a double agent for the Japanese."

"Where did he get that idea?"

"It's too difficult to explain. He says that the old man had secrets and that he was afraid of something."

"He wasn't afraid of the Japanese," he said.

"What *was* he afraid of?"

"Why should I tell you?"

I took the key from my pocket and held it up. "This was in a safe in Johnny's apartment. Have you ever seen it before?"

Ray glanced at it. "No."

"Did you know about the safe?"

He shook his head slowly. Then, after a moment, he said, "Look, I might know who broke into the apartment. A guy might have followed me here to California, but I could be wrong."

"Who is this guy? What was he looking for? You must know, or you wouldn't have driven all the way across six states from Kentucky."

Ray got up and walked to a window, pushing his hands into the pockets of his trousers. "I'm not answering any more questions," he said.

I got up and followed him to the window where I could watch his face. "Maybe Johnny never served in the Air Force," I said.

Ray started to say something but stopped.

"Do you want to hear what I think?" I said. "I think that maybe Johnny was in prison."

"You can think anything that you want," Ray said, after a minute.

"You're not going to help me?"

"No," he said.

I moved away from the window. "I live on Albanil—the street around the corner from Johnny's apartment. My apartment is the fifth building along the street. Come and see me when you're ready to talk." I went towards the door.

"I don't understand," he said. "Why are you so interested in Johnny?"

I looked back at him. "I have an idea, and I'd like to know if I'm right."

———

Late that afternoon, I walked to Rosie's restaurant for something to eat. There were only a few customers, but soon after I sat down, I saw Babe and Bucky come through the door.

"Where's your dad, Bucky?" I said. "I want to talk to him."

"He'll be here later," Bucky said. "Babe and I are going to sit at the bar and watch the six o'clock news on TV until he gets here."

Chester arrived at 6:35 p.m. By then, the place was full of customers and very noisy. It wasn't a good time to try to talk about Johnny, so I paid for my meal and went home.

Nell was in Henry's kitchen and waved to me as I went past the window. I opened the door and said, "Hi, Nell. How are you?"

She was cleaning Henry's kitchen floor. "Come in, Kinsey, it's good to see you," she said. She opened one of the kitchen cabinet doors. "Now then, I—oh, Henry doesn't have any more floor cleaner."

"Shall I go to the supermarket and get you some?" I said.

"Yes, please," she said. "We need some milk, too."

"It's no problem," I told her. "I'll be back soon."

My car—an old cream-colored Volkswagen—was parked nearby. A minute or two later, I drove away.

At the corner of Albanil and Bay streets, I turned right, passing Bucky's cottage. I looked towards the garage apartment and saw that a light was on in one room. I saw the shadow of a person move across the windows.

I slowed the car and stopped. I didn't think that any of the Lees were home. They were at Rosie's restaurant.

Then suddenly, the light went out and the person came out of the apartment. Well, this was interesting.

I saw a parking place, moved my car into it, and switched off the engine.

A man came out of Bucky's driveway with a large duffel bag[42] in his right hand. He had long, dark, curly hair, and he wore dark-colored clothes. I watched him go across the street to a white Ford Taurus. He unlocked the driver's door of the car, pushed the duffle bag across to the passenger seat, and got in. He looked at himself in the driving mirror, smoothed his hair down, and put a Stetson[43] on his head. Next, he switched on his car's headlights and drove away.

I started my Volkswagen and drove after him.

4

The Man in the Stetson

I could clearly see the black Stetson on the man in the Taurus in front of me and I followed him easily.

While I drove with my left hand, I took some paper and a pen from my shoulder bag and wrote down the license plate number[44] of the Taurus. The words PENNY-CAR-RENTAL[45] were also on the license plate.

At 7:17 p.m. the Taurus stopped at the Capri Motel[46]. The motel was small, with only two lines of small cottages, each with a carport[47] at the side. Most of the cottages were empty—there were no lights on inside the rooms and no cars in the carports. But the first two cottages on the left were occupied. The Taurus stopped outside the second cottage on the right.

The man in the Stetson got out of the Taurus, locked the doors, and walked to the front of the cottage. I waited until he was inside. Then I parked the Volkswagen in the carport of an empty cottage opposite and switched off my car's lights.

How long should I wait? I had promised Nell that I would be back soon from the supermarket. And what was in the man's duffel bag—burglars' tools? Was he the same guy who broke into Johnny's apartment?

I had just decided to make a note of the motel's address and go home, when the man came out of the cottage with a woman. She was carrying the duffel bag now. The man was still wearing his Stetson. He put a suitcase in the trunk[48] of the Taurus and she gave him the duffel bag to put with it. Then she got into the passenger side of the car.

I waited until the couple drove away. Then I switched on my car's lights and followed them. They drove to the freeway[49] and then traveled north. After a few miles, they took the exit that went to Santa Teresa airport.

I waited for the couple to park the Taurus in the airport parking lot[50] and buy their parking ticket[51] from a machine. Then I went into the parking lot myself. I got my ticket, parked my car, and watched them walk toward the airport terminal[52]. Then I locked my car and followed them. When I got inside the building, the couple had disappeared into the crowd. I walked through the main lobby and looked around me. Suddenly, I saw the black Stetson! The guy was in the gift shop, paying for some magazines. He wore cowboy boots and a dark-colored wool jacket. He was in his fifties, with a thin face, small dark eyes and a moustache. I could also see that there were gray hairs in the dark hairs of his head and moustache.

The man put the magazines under his arm and turned toward me. There were some public phone booths[53] behind me. I quickly went into the first booth and opened the phone book. I was looking for Bucky's phone number when the guy came out of the gift shop. I watched him go across the lobby. Then I saw the woman at a ticket counter[54]. She had her back toward me and she was carrying a raincoat. The duffel bag was beside her feet and the suitcase was on the conveyor belt[55] next to the ticket agent[56].

I watched the woman give the ticket agent some money and the suitcase moved along the conveyor belt. The woman picked up her ticket and turned to the guy in the Stetson. She was pregnant[57] and much younger than him—early to mid-thirties. Her brown hair was pulled up into a knot on the top of her head, and she wore a big blue dress with a white T-shirt under it. The guy picked up the duffel bag and the two of them moved away from the ticket counter. They stood talking.

What could I do? These people were going to get on a plane and fly out of the state—*with the duffel bag*. But was the guy a burglar? I couldn't prove this. But what had he been doing in Johnny Lee's apartment?

I looked again at the phone book, found Bucky's number, and called him.

Chester answered the phone. "Who's this?" he said.

"Kinsey. I—"

"Get over here!" he said.

"Why, what's happened?" I asked.

"We came home from Rosie's and found Ray Rawson

32

The woman picked up her ticket and turned to the guy in the Stetson.

coming out of Johnny's apartment. He had blood all over his face and two broken fingers. Somebody broke in again and—"

"Wait a second!" I said. A voice was making an announcement in the terminal. Passengers traveling to Palm Beach on American Airlines had to go to Gate 6 and board the plane. I saw the guy pick up the duffel bag, then he and the pregnant woman went toward Gate 6. "Chester, is Ray OK?" I asked.

"He doesn't look very good," Chester answered. "We've got the cops here and an ambulance is coming. Ray will need to go to the hospital. What's all that noise that I can hear? Where are you?"

"I'm at the airport. I saw a guy come out of Johnny's apartment with a duffel bag."

"What!"

"The guy is about to get on a plane with a young woman. Once he leaves this state with that bag, we've got no proof of anything. What's in that bag, Chester? What did he take from the apartment?"

"I don't know," Chester said. "Listen, Kinsey, *do something.* Where's the plane going?"

"Palm Beach, Florida, with a stop in Dallas, Texas."

"Buy a plane ticket and follow him," Chester said quickly. "I'll pay you later. Call me when you can."

I put the phone down and ran across the lobby to the ticket counter. Were the couple on their way to Dallas or Palm Beach? I didn't know. I used my credit card[58] to buy an American Airlines ticket to Dallas and Palm Beach. Then I ran to Gate 6. I could see the man in the Stetson and the pregnant woman standing together, about six passengers ahead of me. Now she carried the magazines and he had the duffel bag.

When they reached the gate, the guy gave the duffel bag

to the woman and kissed her face. She didn't look at him. He watched her walk through the gate, then he turned and walked toward the exit of the terminal building. He glanced at me as he went past. He had a scar on his chin, a line of white skin starting at his lower lip and continuing down his neck. Was the scar from a knife injury?

I went through the doorway of Gate 6. Ahead of me, I saw the pregnant woman get onto the plane.

I looked at my boarding pass[59]. It said SEAT D, ROW[60] 10. The pregnant woman was sitting in Row 8. The duffel bag and her raincoat were in the luggage compartment[61] above her head. She glanced towards me but I looked the other way and sat down in seat 10D.

After a few minutes, the plane's engines started, it moved away from the terminal building and lifted off into the night sky.

———

What was I going to do when the plane landed? I couldn't follow the woman out of the country because I didn't have my passport[62] with me. In fact, the only things that I had were the clothes that I was wearing and my shoulder bag.

I took everything out of my bag and looked at what I had. I had a return plane ticket from Santa Teresa to Palm Beach, a credit card, forty-six dollars and fifty-two cents in cash, my driver's license, my private investigator's license, a phone charge card[63], a comb, a pair of sunglasses, a clean pair of underpants, a small knife, two pens, a bottle of aspirin, a toothbrush and a tube of toothpaste, a lipstick, and a piece of paper. I'd used the paper to write down the license plate number of the Ford Taurus rental car.

After forty-five minutes, the young woman walked past my seat to one of the toilets at the back of the plane. I looked at the other passengers near me. Most of them were asleep or reading. As soon as the woman closed the door of the toilet,

I got up from my seat and moved forward to Row 8. The young woman had taken her handbag with her, but there was a book in the empty seat next to hers. She had used her boarding pass to mark the place where she had finished reading. I quickly put the boarding pass in my pocket and returned to my seat.

Moments later, the pregnant woman walked back to her seat. I saw her pick up the book and begin to search for the boarding pass. After a minute or two she stopped searching, closed her eyes, and went to sleep.

I took her boarding pass from my pocket and looked at it. Her name was Laura Huckaby and she was traveling to Palm Beach.

————

After three hours in the air, we landed in Dallas, Texas. It was 1:45 a.m. (Dallas was two hours ahead of Santa Teresa time.) The plane would stay in Dallas for one hour and ten minutes. Passengers who got off the plane for that short time had to show their boarding passes when they got on again. At Dallas, more fuel was put into the plane and new passengers joined the flight. Laura Huckaby did not have her boarding pass, so I expected her to stay on the plane. She didn't.

Laura took her raincoat and the duffel bag from the compartment over her head. She put the book in the duffel bag and then she left the plane. I followed her. Where was she going? Did she think that we had arrived in Palm Beach?

Dallas airport was quiet at that time of the morning. I followed Laura through a door to the place where passengers collect their luggage. Was her suitcase going all the way to Palm Beach or was it only going as far as Dallas?

I watched her read a notice on a wall. It told her how to call for the small buses that take people to their hotels. She picked up a phone and spoke into it. When she finished the call, I followed her out of the terminal building to the street.

Outside, she stood waiting for one of the hotel buses. The night air was cold. I stood near her but we didn't look at each other. A man in a business suit waited with us. Several buses went past but Laura Huckaby didn't try to stop them. At last, a small red bus with the words DESERT CASTLE written on its side arrived.

Laura lifted her hand and waved at the driver.

The driver stopped the bus and got out. He helped the man with his luggage while Laura Huckaby and I got on the bus. I sat in a seat at the back. Laura sat at the front.

The driver got into his seat and checked the names on his passenger list.

"Wheeler?" he called out.

"Here," replied the man in the business suit.

"Hudson?" the driver said.

To my surprise, Laura Huckaby lifted her hand. *Hudson?* This was interesting. She'd gotten off the plane in Dallas and not Palm Beach. She didn't have her suitcase, she only had the duffel bag. She had booked a hotel room using a different name.

"I'm meeting someone," I told the driver when he looked at me.

5

The Desert Castle, Dallas

We drove around the airport terminal and out onto the freeway. It was very dark and the land was very flat. We passed a few lighted buildings, and then a row of restaurants. Finally, we reached a big hotel, which had the words DESERT

CASTLE written in lights on the outside of the building.

I waited until Laura Huckaby (or Hudson?) and the businessman got out of the bus. Then the three of us walked into the hotel lobby. It was decorated to look like an old English castle.

I was worried about the price of the rooms. I didn't know how long Laura Huckaby would be staying. Maybe I could afford to stay for two nights, but I couldn't pay for more. I now had very little credit on my credit card, and I had only $46.52 in cash.

Laura went to the reception desk, checked in[64], and then went across to the elevators. I saw her go into an elevator and close the doors. Then I watched the red light next to the elevator. The light moved from each number as the elevator went past each floor in the hotel. It stopped at floor twelve. Laura's room must be on the twelfth floor.

I went back to the reception desk and the clerk gave me a form to write my name and address on.

"Everybody's coming in from California tonight," the girl said, smiling. "That other woman flew in from Santa Teresa, too."

"I know," I said. "We're together. Can you put me on the same floor with her?"

The clerk checked her computer screen for a few minutes. Then she said, "I'm sorry, I can't. But you can have a room on floor eight."

"OK," I said. "What's her room number?"

The girl smiled again. "I'm sorry," she said. "I can't give you that information, but phone her when you get to your room. The hotel phone operator will be happy to connect you."

My room did not look like an old English castle. It looked like a bad western movie. The walls and the furniture were decorated in brown and orange colors, and the cover on the bed had pictures of cactuses[65] on it. In the bathroom, the shower curtain was covered with pictures of guns, horses and Stetsons. Near the bed, there was a kettle, a cup and saucer, and some tea, coffee and milk so that I could make a hot drink. There were also some bottles of water, some sweets and a sewing kit[66].

I phoned American Airlines. There were no flights from Dallas to Palm Beach until later that day. So Laura should be staying for the night. I took off my clothes and went to bed. I fell asleep immediately.

———

I woke at midday and phoned Henry. "I'm in Dallas," I told him.

"That doesn't surprise me," he said. "I talked to Chester this morning. He told me that you were following a couple with a duffel bag."

"Yes," I said. "At Santa Teresa airport, the man gave the duffel bag to the woman—she's either his wife or his girlfriend. She bought a ticket to Palm Beach, but she got off the plane in Dallas. I did, too. The man didn't fly with her, but maybe he'll meet her here. Henry, please ask the police in Santa Teresa to check the Capri Motel. The man could be there now."

"OK," Henry said.

"What was stolen from Johnny's apartment last night?" I asked. "Does anybody know?"

"I don't think so," Henry replied. "But the Lees found a hiding place at the bottom of the old man's kitchen cabinet. Somebody had opened it and it's empty now. Maybe the hiding place was empty before, Chester doesn't know. He never saw it before."

"What was Johnny hiding?"

"Chester thinks that the old man was hiding secret documents from the war," Henry said.

"I can't believe that, but I'll try to find out," I said. "What about Ray Rawson?" I asked. "Did the police talk to him?"

"Yes. But he wouldn't tell them anything," Henry said. "Somebody beat Ray Rawson and made him tell them about the hiding place in the apartment. That's what I'm guessing. Ray went to the hospital, but after the doctor treated his injuries, Ray disappeared. Bucky went to Ray's room at the Lexington Hotel, but he's checked out."

I told Henry the telephone number of the Desert Castle hotel. "I'm going to wait and see what the girl does," I said. "If she goes back to the airport and gets on a plane to Palm Beach, I'll get on the plane too."

"Be careful, Kinsey," Henry said.

———

I went downstairs and looked around the lobby. There was a gift shop and a coffee shop next to the reception. It was Saturday and the hotel offices were shut until Monday. At the reception desk I spoke to one of the clerks. I pretended to be a business manager. "Is your sales manager[67] here today?" I asked him. "My company is looking for a hotel in Dallas where we can have a big meeting next spring."

The clerk was a helpful young man. He smiled. "Jillian Brace is our sales manager," he said politely. "But she doesn't work on the weekend."

"Oh," I said. "I have to catch a plane at six o'clock this evening. Can you give me her business card? I can call her from Chicago."

"OK," he said.

"Oh, and my boss wants to know about security[68] here in the hotel," I said.

"Mr Pauley is our security manager. I'll get his card, too."

The clerk went away and came back with the business cards. I thanked him, then I went to one of the lobby phone booths. I asked the hotel phone operator to connect me with

Laura Hudson's room. A woman answered after the phone rang only once.

"Farley?" Laura sounded anxious.

Farley? Was he the guy with the Stetson who was with her in Santa Teresa airport?

"Ms[69] Hudson?" I said. I pretended to be a member of the hotel staff. I gave myself a false name. "I'm Sara Fullerton, Jillian Brace's assistant in the sales office here in the Desert Castle. Can I ask you a few questions? It won't take more than two minutes."

"OK, but please be quick," Laura said. "I'm waiting for a call."

"Thank you," I said. "Our hotel register shows that you arrived last night from Santa Teresa, California, on American Airlines flight 508. Is that correct?"

"Y–yes," she said.

"Did you have any trouble getting a bus to the hotel?"

"No, I just picked up the phone at the airport and asked for the Desert Castle bus."

"Was the driver polite and helpful?"

"Yes."

"We're pleased to hear that," I said. "How long will you be staying with us?"

"I don't know yet," she said. "Certainly one more night. After that, I'm not sure."

"Thank you, Ms Hudson. Now, your room number is…"

"I'm in 1236," she said.

"Yes, that's the information that we have on our register. Thank you again, Ms Hudson. We hope that you enjoy your stay with us."

Now I needed to get into her room. I went for a second walk around the lobby and found a door with the words EMPLOYEES ONLY written on it. I pushed the door open and went down some fire stairs[70] to another door with the sign, NO

41

ENTRY. This door wasn't locked and I stepped into a corridor where the air was much warmer and smelled of cooked food and machinery. To my left, wide metal doors were open and I could see some big trucks parked outside. There were security cameras over the doors, so I walked the other way. I turned a corner and went into the first of several kitchens. I walked past people who were preparing food. There were strong smells of cooking food and it was very hot. It was good to get out into the main corridor.

Ahead of me, a line of linen carts[71] was against one wall. The carts were filled with sheets and towels. I walked past them, and along the corridor until I came to a door with the sign, EMPLOYEE LINENS. I opened it. Inside the room there were several hundred red uniforms hanging on rails. The uniforms had been cleaned and they were ready for the hotel employees to collect.

"Hello?" I said loudly. There was no answer.

I began looking through the uniforms on the rail. On each one, there was a name on a piece of paper—Lucy, Historia, Juanita, Lateesha, Mary, Gloria, Nettie. I took three uniforms from their metal hangers and went back into the corridor.

"What are you doing?" a voice behind me said. It was a woman in a red uniform. "I'm Mrs Spitz, the Linen Manager."

"Oh, Mrs Spitz!" I said quickly. "I was looking for you. I'm Jillian Brace's assistant." I pulled a business card from my pocket and she took it from my hand.

"This says Burnham J. Pauley," she said. She looked at me. "What's happening here?"

"Well," I said. "I'm glad you asked. Because—er—the hotel is thinking about getting some new uniforms. And Mr Pauley asked me to show him some that we're using now."

"That's stupid!" said Mrs Spitz. "We only just got those uniforms. What's your name?"

"Vikki Biggs," I lied.

She pointed a finger at me. "Don't move. I'm going to find out about this. What's Ms Brace's phone number?"

"It's 202," I said.

Mrs Spitz went into the uniforms room and the door closed behind her. I walked away quickly, carrying the three uniforms over my left arm. I found the stairs and ran up them.

When I got to my room on the eighth floor, I dropped the uniforms onto a chair and fell onto the bed. When my breathing was normal again, I got up and put on the stolen uniforms, one at a time. The skirts were too large, but the first uniform fitted me OK. I put my jeans on again and put the uniform in the clothes closet. I pushed the other two uniforms into a drawer in the desk.

I checked my money. I could just afford to buy some lunch. A waiter delivered it to my room. At two o'clock I went out into the corridor. At one end of the corridor there was a space with shelves full of sheets, towels and cleaning things. Two linen carts were in front of the shelves.

I went down to the gift shop in the lobby and bought a book to read. Then I took the phone charge card out of my pocket, went to a phone booth, and called Laura's room. When she answered, I said, "Sorry, wrong number," and put the phone down.

————

I stayed in my room and read my book for most of the afternoon. Then I made a cup of coffee and ate the sweets. Soon after seven o'clock, I put on a red hotel uniform, put my room key in my pocket, and went up the fire stairs to floor twelve.

The place on the twelfth floor for the sheets, towels and cleaning things was the same as on floor eight. I took a vacuum cleaner and began to clean the floor.

At 7:36 p.m. a waiter took some food on a tray to Laura's room. He came out a few minuites later and went past me to the elevator. During the next half hour, people passed me but they didn't look at me. Then I put the vacuum cleaner back with the cleaning things and took some clean towels from a shelf.

I walked to room 1236 and knocked on the door. A few seconds later, Laura opened it. "Yes?" she said.

"I'm here to get your bed ready for the night," I said.

"OK," she said, and stepped back to let me enter.

I put clean towels in the bathroom, then I pulled the drapes across the windows. Laura's room key was on the desk. I immediately began to think of a plan to get it.

Laura sat down at the desk to read a magazine and I saw bruises[72] on her legs. Did her boyfriend in the Stetson beat her? I thought that he'd probably beaten Ray Rawson too.

Laura's dinner things were on a tray on the desk. A white cloth was lying on top of the dirty plates.

I turned back the cover on the bed, and then opened the closet door. There was the duffel bag.

"What are you doing?" Laura asked quickly.

"Do you need more hangers for your clothes?" I said.

"No, thank you."

I closed the closet door and picked up the rest of the clean towels. "Shall I take the dinner tray?" I asked.

She glanced at the desk. "Yes, please."

I put down the towels and went across to the desk. I picked up Laura's room key and hid it under the white cloth. Then I took the tray to the door and put it outside, on the corridor floor. Laura waited for me to get the towels, then she gave me five dollars.

"Thank you," I said as I left the room.

After she closed the door, I picked up her key from the dinner tray and went back to my room.

44

I opened the closet door. There was the duffel bag.

6

Ray Rawson

I got back to my room and had a shower. Then Henry phoned. "Have you heard from Ray Rawson?" he asked.

"No," I said. "I thought that he'd disappeared."

"He came back," Henry said. "He went to the Lees' house and Bucky told him what was happening. Bucky knew that you'd left town, but he didn't know where you were. Then Ray came over to my house. I was out, but he saw Charlie. Ray told Charlie that you were in danger. And he also said something about a key."

"He probably talked about the key that Johnny had in his safe," I said.

"Bucky told Ray that you had it with you," Henry said.

"I do," I said. "Why? You sound worried."

"I am worried, but not about that. When Ray came to my house, he told Charlie that you needed help. So Charlie gave him the name of your hotel in Dallas."

Now I began to get worried. "How did he know the name of this hotel?"

"I wrote it down and Charlie found the note."

"Does Ray know my room number, too?" I asked.

"Yes, I'm sorry," Henry replied. "I don't think that Ray will fly all the way to Dallas, but he'll probably phone you. I wanted to warn[73] you. I'm worried about this, Kinsey, but there's nothing that I can do."

"Stop worrying, Henry, but thanks for the warning."

After I put down the phone, I thought about moving to a different room, but then I remembered Mrs Spitz. She must have described me to the hotel security staff. They were probably looking for me now. It would be stupid to go down to the desk and show my face. And I didn't want to leave the hotel now that I had a key to Laura Huckaby's room.

Then I remembered the key from Johnny's safe. I took the heavy iron key from my shoulder bag and looked at it. In the morning I could mail it to Henry, but I needed a hiding place until then.

After thinking for a second or two, I took a pair of scissors from the sewing kit and cut a hole in the lining[74] of my jacket. I pushed the key inside the lining and then sewed up the lining with a needle and thread.

That night, I slept in my clothes. I was ready to leave the hotel quickly, at any time.

————

The phone rang and woke me at 8 a.m. I almost jumped out of the bed.

"Who is it?" I said into the phone.

"Oh, I'm sorry. Did I wake you? This is Ray."

I sat on the side of the bed and rubbed my hand across my eyes. "Where are you?" I asked.

"I'm here, at the Desert Castle. I'm in the lobby," he said. "I've got to talk to you. Can I come up to your room?"

"No," I said. "I'll meet you in the hotel's coffee shop in...in fifteen minutes."

I washed, got dressed again, and put the two room keys— mine and Laura Huckaby's—in my pocket. Then I went down to the lobby.

Ray Rawson was waiting in the coffee shop. He looked awful. There were bruises on his face and he had bandages across his nose, and across three fingers on his right hand.

"When did you get here?" I asked him.

"Three-thirty this morning," he said. "I got a rental car at the airport and drove here."

"Have you booked a room?"

"Yeah, number 1006."

47

The waitress came with our cups of coffee.

"Have some breakfast," Ray said to me. "I'll pay."

"OK," I replied. I was hungry and I didn't have enough money to buy food. "I'll have coffee, orange juice, eggs and toast."

"I'll have the same," Ray told the waitress. After she went away, he said, "Do you have the key that Bucky took from Johnny's safe?"

Why should I tell Ray anything? He hadn't given me any information.

"I don't have it with me," I said. "but I know where it is. Why did you tell Charlie Pitts that I was in danger because of the key? I talked to Henry last night, and he told me what you said to his brother."

"I never said that you were in danger," Ray said. "Maybe the old guy didn't hear me clearly."

"OK, let's talk about something else."

"You were right about Johnny," Ray said after a minute or two. "He was never in the Air Force. He was in jail. That's where we met. But we didn't meet in 1942, it was earlier. Maybe 1939, or 1940. We were arrested by the police in Louisville because we'd gotten drunk and started fighting. I was nineteen.

"Neither of us served during the war—we were not allowed to fight," Ray said. "We didn't pass the medical examinations. I had two broken eardrums[75] and a bad knee. I can't remember what was wrong with Johnny. Anyway, we were bored, so we started breaking into places. After a time, we were caught by the police and we went to jail. Johnny went to jail in Lexington. I went to a jail in Louisville. When Johnny got out of jail two years later, he moved his family to California."

"What happened to you?" I asked.

"I've been in and out of different jails for the last forty

years," he replied. "I did some bad things, but I never killed anybody.

"In the 1940s I was out of jail long enough to marry a girl called Marla," Ray continued. "We had a daughter, but I haven't seen her for a long time. After I'd spent several years in different jails, Marla and I got divorced. I became a criminal when I met Johnny. Maybe he thought that it was his fault."

"Is that why he wrote to you for forty years?" I said.

"Maybe. Or maybe because his wife and I were the only people who knew that he'd been in jail. He told stories about his life during the war. But he got all those stories from books. He pretended that he was a fighter pilot in the Air Force. His kids thought that he was a hero, but he knew that the stories were lies. And so did I."

"It must be strange to be out of prison after all that time," I said.

"Yeah," he said. "I'd like to go back to Louisville and see my mother again. She's eighty-five, but she's a tough old lady."

"How old are you?" I asked.

"Sixty-five," he said. "I wrote to Johnny in April. He told me to come to California as soon as I got out of jail. He said that he'd help me. He had some ideas about a small business we could both start.

"I came out of jail three weeks ago. I didn't know that Johnny was dead until I knocked at Bucky's door."

"Who is the guy who broke into Johnny's place?" I asked.

"His name is Gilbert Hays. He was in jail with me two years ago. I told him about Johnny. I said that Johnny was always hiding cash somewhere in his apartment."

"Were you planning to steal Johnny's money?"

"No! I wouldn't do that. But Gilbert probably followed me to California after I got out of jail. When you told me about the first break-in, I knew that he was the burglar."

"How did you know that Johnny had money hidden somewhere in his apartment?"

"I *didn't* know for sure," Ray replied. "But Johnny died suddenly. He didn't have time to hide his money anywhere else. When I talked to Bucky, I realized that he didn't have any of Johnny's money. So, if there is any money, its probably still in the apartment. I decided to rent the place, so that I could try and find it."

"Did you tell Bucky about the money?" I asked.

"No!" Ray said. "But if I do find it, maybe I can ask the Lees for some of it. There will still be plenty left for them." He smiled.

"How did Gilbert Hays know Johnny's address?"

Ray showed me his broken fingers. "Because I told him before he broke every bone in my hand."

"How did you know where the money was hidden?"

"I knew the kind of hiding places that Johnny would choose." He looked at me. "You don't believe me."

I smiled. "You tell lies as well as I do."

"Let's stop worrying about the past," he said, "and think about what to do next."

"Ah, so now *we're* working together, are we?"

"Yeah, sure. Gilbert Hays took Johnny's money, and I want it back. Not just for me, but for Bucky and Chester. Isn't that why they hired you? To return what Hays stole?"

I hesitated. "Well…yes."

"So, what's the plan?" asked Ray.

He was telling me lies, I knew that. But what was the truth? I didn't know. I took Laura's hotel key out of my pocket and put it on the table.

"That's the key to Laura Huckaby's room," I said. "She's the woman with the duffel bag. She's using a false name— Laura Hudson."

I was wearing a hotel maid's uniform again. I put towels and sheets into one of the linen carts on Laura Huckaby's floor, then I pushed it ahead of me down the corridor.

This was my plan. Ray Rawson was going to call Laura from a phone in the lobby. He was going to pretend to be the clerk. Ray would tell Laura that there was a parcel for her at the reception desk and he'd ask her to collect it as soon as possible. When Laura went to the lobby, I'd use her key to get into room 1236. At the desk, the real clerk would search for a parcel that wasn't there. When Laura left the desk to come upstairs again, Ray would warn me. He'd call room 1236 and let the phone ring once. That's when I would get out of the room, if I was still there.

I knew where to find the duffel bag and I could empty it in ten seconds. Then I would go back to my room, put on my own clothes, and meet Ray in the lobby. We could be on

51

our way to the airport before Laura realized that anything had happened.

At 10 a.m. I was standing in the corridor outside Laura's room. I heard her phone ring twice. I waited. Where was she? At 10:17 a.m. she came out of her room. I was folding towels and putting them into the linen cart when she saw me.

"Oh, hello," she said. "Did you see my key in my room last night?"

"No, I didn't," I said. "Have you lost it? You can always get another from the reception desk."

"OK, thanks," she said.

She walked towards the elevators. When she turned the corner, I put down the towels. As soon as I heard the doors of the elevator close, I unlocked the door of room 1236 and went inside. It was 10:18 a.m.

7

Laura

The duffel bag was in the clothes closet with Laura's handbag beside it. I opened the duffel bag and found some clean clothes and underwear inside. There was no money.

I searched the handbag next. There were papers, credit cards, and about one hundred dollars in cash. I put the duffel bag and the handbag back in the closet and I checked the closet shelf. Empty. I put my hand inside the pockets of Laura's raincoat, and the pockets of the dress next to it. They were empty. I checked the bathroom, then looked in all the desk drawers in the main room. Nothing.

Suddenly, the phone rang once and then it went silent. Laura Huckaby was on her way back to the room! I looked under and inside both the beds. I searched the duffel bag again. *Nothing.* I grabbed[76] the duffel bag and ran to the door.

I heard the elevator doors open when I shut the door to Laura's room door. I dropped the duffel bag into the linen cart, pulled some sheets over it, and pushed the cart down the corridor.

Laura Huckaby went past me, walking fast. She had a room key in her hand. She opened the door to room 1236 and went inside. I pushed the cart into its place at the end of the corridor, pulled out the duffel bag, and hurried to the fire stairs.

I reached the eighth floor and started walking towards room 815. I stopped. A man in a business suit was standing outside my room. He looked like the hotel manager. I watched him knock on the door. After a moment, he took a key out of his pocket, unlocked the door and went inside.

I went to the space where the linen cart stood in the corridor of Floor 8. I hid the duffel bag in a large bag for dirty linen, then began counting the clean sheets. I had to do something while I waited for the manager to come out of my room.

I heard the door to the fire stairs open and close. A moment later, a security man was standing beside me.

"What are you doing?" he asked.

"Mrs Spitz told me to check the linen here," I said.

He looked at me carefully. "What's your name?"

"Katy," I said. "I'm new. Were you looking for the manager? I think he's in 815."

"Mr Denton is on this floor?" he asked.

Was that the manager's name? I didn't know. "Yes," I said. "I think he's looking for that strange guest, but she just left."

"How long ago did she leave?"

"About five minutes ago," I said. "I got off the elevator when she got on."

The security man walked down the corridor and knocked on my door. After a moment, it opened. The two men spoke for a minute, then they went to the elevator. I waited until I heard the elevator doors close. Then I took the duffel bag from its hiding place and I ran to my room.

I changed into my own clothes and pushed the red uniform into the duffel bag. Then I left the room quickly and ran down the fire stairs to the lobby. I couldn't see Mr Denton, or the security man, or Ray Rawson. I had arranged to meet Ray by the lobby phones, but he wasn't there.

I walked into the ladies' restroom[77] and emptied the duffel bag. I looked for another compartment inside the bag, but there wasn't one.

I went back into the lobby and across to one of the four public phones. I took my phone charge card from my jacket pocket and I checked how much money I had. There were some coins and the five-dollar bill[78] that Laura had given me the night before. I used the charge card to call Chester.

"I've got the duffel bag," I told him. "There's nothing important in it. If Laura and Gilbert stole something from the apartment and put it in the bag, it isn't there now. Maybe they moved what they found to somewhere else. Did you ever *see* any cash in Johnny's apartment?"

"No, but—"

"Maybe Gilbert broke into the apartment and didn't find anything," I said.

"Listen," Chester said angrily. "I'm paying for you to fly all the way to Dallas. So I expect you to find what was stolen from my dad's apartment."

"Wait a minute," I said. "You haven't paid me anything yet."

"No, and I'm not going to pay you now. You can stop working on this case. I don't need you any more!" He banged down the phone.

I wanted to scream with anger, but instead I opened the phone book to find the number for American Airlines. I picked up the five dollar bill. Was this the only money that I was going to get for this job? Then I looked carefully at the bill. It was very old. The date 1934 was printed on it. How did Laura Huckaby get a bill as old as that? And did she have more old money?

I closed the phone book. Maybe this case wasn't finished yet. Maybe I was finding some answers now.

The door behind me opened suddenly. Before I could turn around, somebody pulled me out of the phone booth.

55

"Where have you been?" whispered Ray. He pushed me across the lobby and through the emergency door to the fire stairs.

"Where have *you* been?" I said.

"A security guy has been asking me questions. He knows who you are. He wants to know what you're doing here."

"Why did he ask you?" I said.

"The waitress in the coffee shop saw us together," Ray said. "The security guy talked to her. He described me and asked her questions about me. So I told him that you're a private detective. I said that we're working on a case together. I told him that I couldn't talk about it."

"Does the security guy think that you're a cop[79]?"

"No, but the people in security don't care about me. They just want me to leave the Desert Castle. Is that the duffel bag? Give it to me."

I pulled it away from him. "Are you telling me the truth, Ray? Are we looking for cash? Or are we looking for drugs, diamonds, or stolen documents?"

"Money. Did you find it?"

"No, nothing. How much money?"

"Eight thousand dollars, maybe a little less by now."

"Is that *all*?" I said. "Where did it come from?"

"I'll tell you later. Let's get out of here," Ray said.

"Wait. We need a plan," I said. "The cash isn't in Laura's room because I've searched it."

"Then she must have it with her," he said.

"No, she—" And then I had an idea. "Wait a minute. I think I know where the money is. Come with me."

———

I knocked on the door of room 1236. Ray stood behind me, against the wall and to the left of Laura's door.

"Hi," I said when she opened it. "I found this in the hallway. I think it's yours."

She looked at the duffle bag suspiciously[80]. "You found it in the hall? How did it get there?"

"I don't know," I said.

"Well, thanks," she said, and held out her hand.

I pushed the door open quickly and walked into the room. Ray came in after me.

"Hey!" she said.

"We need to talk," I said. "My name is Kinsey Millhone. This is my friend, Ray. We want to talk about the money."

She moved quickly to the phone but Ray took it away from her.

"Who are you?" she said, a little frightened now.

"We followed you from California," I said. "Your friend, Gilbert, stole some money. Ray wants it back."

She looked at Ray and said, "You're Ray Rawson!"

"Just give us the money," he said, "then we'll leave."

"It isn't yours," Laura said. "It belongs to Gilbert."

"No," Ray said. "It belongs to me and a guy named Johnny Lee, who died four months ago."

"That's not true!" Laura shouted. "The money is Gilbert's, and you know it. You told the cops about the robbery. Gilbert's brother, Donnie, was killed by the cops because of you."

"Wait a minute?" I said. "What robbery?"

Ray didn't answer me. "Gilbert lied to you," he told Laura. "Do you want to hear the truth?"

"Stop!" I said. "Do you two know each other?"

Ray looked at me. "This is my daughter," he said. "I haven't seen her for years."

Laura jumped toward Ray. She started crying and hitting him on the chest. He put his arms around her and held her tightly.

"I'm sorry, baby[81]," he said. "I feel so bad about everything."

8

The Bank Robbery

I watched Ray and Laura with my mouth open. Then I went and looked out the window until Laura stopped crying.

Suddenly, I walked across the room and knocked Laura's stomach with my hand. She cried out in surprise. And then I was sure. "You're not pregnant, are you?" I said.

"Hey, what are you doing?" Ray said.

"She's hiding the money under her dress," I said. "It's in some kind of bag or a vest. That's not a baby in her stomach, it's the money. She's pretending to be pregnant."

"I *am* pregnant," Laura said angrily.

"Pull up your dress and we'll check your stomach," I said. "I could hit you in the stomach again, but harder." I lifted my hand.

"OK!" Laura shouted. "All right, the money is in a vest under my dress!"

"Good, let's see it," I said.

"Ray, tell her to get away from me," she said.

Ray looked at me. "Stop this." He looked at his daughter. "You start the story. What did Gilbert tell you?"

Laura sat down on the bed. "There was a bank robbery in 1941. There were five robbers—you, Gilbert, his brother Donnie, Johnny Lee, and a man named McDermid."

"No, six of us robbed the bank," Ray said. "There were two McDermid brothers, Frank and Darrell."

"Gilbert says that you told the cops about the robbery," Laura said. "The cops arrived in the middle of the robbery. There was some shooting and Donnie Hays was killed. Frank McDermid and a cop died too. The money disappeared, but Gilbert was sure that you and Johnny knew where it was hidden. Johnny was in jail for two years. When he got out, he disappeared. Gilbert waited until you got out of jail, Ray. Then he followed you to Johnny's apartment. He found the money that was left from the robbery. Gilbert says that it's his money."

"Laura, can I ask something?" I said. "Did Marla, your mother, tell you when Ray was getting out of prison?"

She nodded and said, "Yeah."

"Baby," Ray said to her. "Don't you understand? Gilbert wanted to find me, so he started a relationship with you."

"No," she said. "That *isn't* true."

"Did Gilbert ask about me quite soon after your relationship started?" Ray said. "Laura, think about it. More than forty years ago, Gilbert and I rob a bank. Then Gilbert just 'arrives' at your home one day and says that he loves you. Didn't you think that it was strange? You say that I told the cops about the robbery. If I did tell them, why did I spend forty years in jail? I would have said to the cops, 'If I go to jail, I won't tell you the names of the other robbers.'

"Johnny always thought that Darrell McDermid told the cops about the robbery," Ray went on. "Darrell was in jail for only one year. Laura, Gilbert wants all the money for himself. He also wants to blame me because Frank died. Are you and Gilbert Hays married?"

"N—no, but we live together," Laura said.

Ray looked at the bruises on her legs but said nothing about them. "OK, now let me tell you my story," he said. "It starts in the winter of 1937. A lot of rain fell in Kentucky that year, and the water in the Ohio River rose up and flooded the land.

"Johnny was in jail in Lexington when sixty of the prisoners escaped," Ray said. "He was one of the men who escaped. He got as far as Louisville and saw the flood. He made a boat and started to help people.

"Lots of buildings in Lexington were destroyed during the flood," Ray went on. "When the river water went down again, the town officials paid men to repair anything that was broken. Johnny was one of these men. He was paid to work on the buildings. One day, he was looking at a building with a crack in one wall. Suddenly he realized that the building was a bank. But Johnny didn't repair the wall. He just covered up the crack. Everybody was too busy to notice this.

"Johnny and I met four years later," Ray said. "He told me how we could rob the bank. But he knew that we needed help with the bank's alarm[82]. I knew Donnie Hays, so I asked him to work with us. Donnie knew about alarms. He brought his brother, Gilbert, with him. Johnny also asked two guys named McDermid to help us. Well, Donnie Hays turned off the bank's alarm and we got in."

"Wait a minute," I said. "Laura thought that someone called Farley was phoning her yesterday. Who's Farley?"

"Gilbert's nephew," Laura said. "The three of us came to California together."

Ray went on with his story. "We started taking the cash and other valuable things from the safe in the bank. Everything was going OK until the cops suddenly arrived. There was a lot of shooting and Donnie Hays, Frank McDermid, and a cop were killed. I killed the cop. The cops caught Darrell McDermid and Gilbert, but Johnny and I escaped. Johnny said that he had a perfect place to hide the cash and valuables. But he said that it would be better if only one of us knew the hiding place. Well, we separated, and by the time the cops caught us, Johnny had hidden everything. The cops beat Johnny, but he didn't tell them where the money and valuables were. He only said that he had robbed the bank.

"Me and Johnny were sent to jail for twenty-five years," Ray went on. "But Johnny's lawyer made an appeal to the

"*Suddenly he realized that the building was a bank.*"

court. The police had beaten Johnny to make him talk about the robbery. When he heard about this, the judge said that Johnny's arrest was illegal. So Johnny was released from jail after two years and he went home to his family. Later, he removed some of the cash from where it was hidden for his family and my mother."

He pointed at Laura's stomach. "That's what's left of the money," he said.

"How can you be sure that it's $8000?" I asked.

"Because Johnny told me how much he took and how much he spent."

"Where are the rest of the valuables from the bank?" I asked.

"I don't know," Ray replied. "Johnny never told me."

Laura began to cry loudly.

"What's wrong?" Ray asked.

"I thought that there would be more money," she said.

"Laura's OK, Ray," I said. "Do you know what I think? I think that she and Farley, Gilbert's nephew, are working together now. She's run away from Gilbert, with the money. That's my guess."

"Is that right?" said Ray. He was worried now. He knew that Gilbert was dangerous.

Laura nodded, tears were running down her face. "Yes. Farley loves me. He knows that Gilbert beats me. I have to get away before he kills me."

"Gilbert is crazy," Ray said. "Why do you stay with him?"

"I've tried to get away from him but he always finds me," Laura went on. "He won't let me work. He won't let me have any money of my own. This is my only chance to escape from him."

"Take the $8000," Ray said to her.

"No, I'll talk to Farley," said Laura, rubbing her hand across her eyes. "We'll make a new plan. I thought that there would be more money. Gilbert talked about millions of dollars."

"There were never millions," said Ray.

"I was going to a foreign country to hide," Laura said. "Eight thousand dollars isn't going to be enough."

"Go to another state in this country," Ray said. "Change your name. Find work."

"Gilbert will find me."

"Where's Farley now?" I asked her.

"He's in Santa Teresa with Gilbert. We didn't want Gilbert to get suspicious."

"I don't understand," I said.

"When I left Santa Teresa, I was going to fly to Palm Beach, Florida," Laura explained. "Gilbert has a friend there. He paid this friend to meet me and stay with me until he and Farley arrived. Gilbert wanted to get the money out of California as soon as possible. But he and Farley had to wait for their passports to arrive. I already had my passport. I was going to wait in Palm Beach for them, then later we would fly to Rio de Janeiro."

"But you got off the plane in Dallas," I said. "When was Farley going to meet you?"

"As soon as he could. He knows where I am. We made an arrangement. Farley was going to call me."

"Did he ever call you?" I asked.

"He called me this morning," she replied. "He had to wait until Gilbert went out of the house. I told him about the money, and he was frightened. He said that he would call me again in an hour."

Ray said, "But he didn't call?"

"No," Laura replied.

"Gilbert's friend in Palm Beach will have called Gilbert," I said. "He'll have told Gilbert that you never arrived in Florida."

"Of course," said Laura, "but Gilbert doesn't know where I am."

"What about Farley?" I said. "Gilbert will see that Farley is frightened, and he'll guess your little plan."

"Of course he will!" Ray said.

"But Dallas is a big place," Laura said. "He won't find me."

"Farley knows where you are," Ray said.

"Well, yeah, but I can trust him," said Laura.

"You've *got* to get out of here, Laura," said Ray.

"No," Laura replied. "I must wait for Farley. I'm staying."

I searched through my shoulder bag for my plane ticket, then I started looking for the phone book. "Well, I'm getting out of here."

"You're leaving us?" Ray said. "What about Chester?"

"I'm not working for Chester any longer, so there's no reason for me to stay. I came to find the cash that you want to give away—the *stolen* cash. And that's another reason for me to leave."

"It's been forty years since we took the money from the bank," said Ray. "The bank closed in 1949. Most of the customers are dead, so who could I return the money to?"

"But you stole the money—that's still a crime," I said.

"What about the statute of limitations[83]?" he said. "The law says that I can't be punished for a forty-year-old crime, doesn't it?"

"Ask a lawyer," I said. "Maybe you're right."

I phoned American Airlines.

"My name is Kinsey Millhone," I told the ticket agent. "I'm in Dallas and I want to fly to Santa Teresa as soon as possible."

The agent told me that there was a flight to Santa Teresa at 2:22 p.m. and another at 6:10 p.m.

"OK," I said. I checked my watch. It was 12:30 p.m. I put down the phone.

"Are you going to fly back to California?" I asked Ray.

"No, I'm going to wait here with Laura until she hears from Farley," he said. "Then I'll go to Louisville."

"What about Chester?" I said. "Half the money belongs to him."

Ray smiled. "I was never going to give him any of the money."

———

I took a taxi to the airport. I didn't get on the 2:22 p.m. flight, so I had to wait four hours.

At five o'clock, the flight from Santa Teresa arrived. I watched the passengers getting off the plane.

Suddenly I saw a black Stetson in the crowd and I recognized the person who was wearing it. It was Gilbert. He was one of the last passengers to leave the plane.

9

The Fire

I had thirty minutes to wait before I could get on my flight to Santa Teresa. I decided to follow Gilbert Hays.

While he waited for his luggage, I used my charge card to phone the Desert Castle. I saw Gilbert collect his bags and go toward the airport lobby.

Suddenly he stopped and opened one of his bags. He pulled a gun from the bag and pushed it into the belt of his jeans. Then he walked across to the car rental desk.

The hotel operator answered my call. "Desert Castle. How can I help you?"

"Please will you ring Laura Hudson's room?" I asked.

"She's in 1236."

Laura's phone was busy. I spoke to the operator again.

"Please ring Ray Rawson's room," I said.

The phone rang in Ray's room fifteen times. He didn't answer.

Gilbert Hays was still at the rental desk. I went out of the airport terminal to the street. I looked around for an airport police officer. I couldn't see one.

A large white car stopped in front of me. The driver got out and opened the doors at the back. Two people with silver-gray hair stepped from the car and took their luggage from the driver.

There were no buses from the Desert Castle hotel and I couldn't see a taxi. I stared at the large white car. The driver got in and was going to drive away. I leaned forward and knocked on the window. It opened and the driver looked at me. He was in his thirties, with a round face and short red hair.

I showed him my private detective's license. "I need help," I said quickly. "There's a guy with a gun in the airport building. He's here to kill two of my friends. I need to get to the Desert Castle hotel. Do you know it?"

He looked carefully at my license. "I know it." He unlocked the passenger door and I got in.

There was a phone inside the car. I pointed to it and said, "Can I use that to call the cops?"

He nodded and we drove away from the airport.

I phoned the police and told them my story. And they said that an officer would meet me at the Desert Castle.

———

There was no police officer at the hotel when I arrived. I took the elevator to the twelfth floor and ran down the hallway to Laura's room. I knocked on the door of 1236.

Laura opened it. "What are you doing here?" she said.

"Where's Ray?" I said quickly. "I saw Gilbert at the airport. He's on his way here with a gun. Go and get your things! Let's get out of here."

Laura's face went white. "Oh, no."

"What's the problem?" Ray said from behind her.

"Go!" I told Laura, and she moved towards the closet.

"She saw Gilbert," she told Ray, as she got her raincoat and the duffel bag from the closet. "He's coming here."

"Do you have a car?" I asked Ray.

"Yeah, a rental car," he said. "It's in the parking lot at the side of the hotel."

"Give me the car keys," I said. "You two wait for me outside, in the hotel driveway. Don't go in the elevators. Go down the fire stairs. I'll get the car and meet you out in the driveway. Gilbert doesn't know me, so it'll be OK if he sees me in the lobby."

Ray described the car and told me the license plate number. Then he and Laura went off to the fire stairs. I used an elevator to go down to the lobby. When the doors opened, Gilbert was standing there, waiting to go up.

For a moment we looked at each other, then I moved to the right and walked past him. Behind me, the elevator doors closed. I checked the lobby for police officers but there were none.

I glanced back at the elevator—and saw the doors open again and Gilbert step out. He stood there, looking at me. Something in his eyes was saying, "I remember you from Santa Teresa airport." How did he connect me with Laura Huckaby? I don't know. But he did.

I walked past the coffee shop and turned into a short corridor with three doors. I pushed through one of them. I was in a hallway where the walls went up into darkness. I passed wooden boxes filled with glasses, carts filled with plates, and piles of chairs.

I went up six stairs. At the top, the corridor continued. Behind me, I heard a door open and shut. I started to run, my shoulder bag hitting against my side. On the wall to my left there was a metal ladder—a fire escape. I glanced back. I could hear someone coming along the corridor behind me.

I started to climb the ladder. My bag felt heavy and it was slowing me down.

At the top of the fire escape, I could touch the ceiling above me. I was standing on a narrow metal catwalk[84], high inside the building. Along the right side of the catwalk, there was a metal chain at the height of my waist. It was the only thing between me and the darkness below. I walked slowly, staying close to the wall.

I came to a small wooden door and opened it. In front of me, there was a lighted corridor about six feet high. There were windows along the top of the corridor wall on the right side, and some were open. I shut the door behind me and went to the nearest window and looked down. Below me there was a large, long room.

I shook the things out of my shoulder bag onto the floor of the corridor. I pushed my driver's license, phone charge card, private investigator's license, credit card, knife, toothbrush and toothpaste, and the keys to Ray's rental car into my jacket pockets. I left the bag on the floor. Now I could move more easily. Then I heard someone walking along the metal catwalk on the other side of the door. I went back to the door and quickly pushed the bolt across.

I'd locked the door just in time. Someone was pushing it.

After a minute or two, I heard the person go back along the catwalk to the ladder. I waited fifteen minutes before I unlocked the door and looked out. At that moment, the fire alarm sounded.

Water sprinklers[85] came on over my head and water began to pour down like rain. I could smell smoke in the air. Then

In front of me, there was a lighted corridor about six feet high.

the lights went out. I moved slowly along the dark catwalk. Ahead of me, I could just see a red glow. Hot smoke was coming up around me. At last I reached the ladder and climbed down. It was wet from the water sprinklers. I could see the red glow of the fire below me and I heard the sound of breaking glass and roaring flames.

At the bottom of the ladder I turned left and, a few feet further on, I saw a door. I pushed it open and found that I was in a dark hallway. The carpet under my feet was wet and, as I walked slowly forward in the dark, I held my hands out in front of me.

Somehow, I found the door to the fire stairs. At the other side of the door, the air smelled cold and clean. I went down the stairs to the first floor of the hotel. All the main rooms were empty. I saw a fire door marked EMERGENCY EXIT and pushed it open. At last, I was outside the building. I walked quickly to the parking lot to find Ray's car.

There were fire engines[86] at the hotel entrance and a crowd of people outside the doors. Flames and black smoke were coming from parts of the hotel. I found Ray's rental car parked in a lot at the side of the hotel and got into it. My clothes and hair were wet and I smelled of smoke.

I drove out of the parking lot and into the driveway. Ray and Laura ran out from behind some trees. Ray threw three bags into the trunk of the car. Then he got into the passenger seat beside me. Laura got into the back seat. She was still wearing the money vest under her dress.

"Kinsey! We were afraid that you wouldn't get out of there," Ray said. He turned and looked at the burning hotel behind us. "Did Gilbert do that?"

"Of course he did!" Laura said.

"Are you going back to the airport?" Ray asked me.

"Not while I look like this," I said. "Anyway, I've missed my plane and—oh, no! I left my plane ticket in my bag!"

"Well, it's gone now," Laura said, half-smiling.

"Where are we going now?" Ray said.

"I don't know," I said. "Where are we? Do you have a map?"

He took a road map from a compartment in the front of the car and switched on the light above his head. "Look for the U.S. 30 highway sign," he said to me. "That road will take us northeast."

"Going to where?" I asked.

Laura glanced over at Ray. "Louisville, right? You think that we should go back there? Gilbert isn't stupid, Ray. Where do you think that *he's* going?"

"OK, so Gilbert might go to Louisville too. But how is he going to find us? It's a twelve-hour trip by car and he'll never know which road we took. We can check into a motel and use false names."

"He found Laura in Dallas," I reminded him.

"He probably made Farley tell him where she was," Ray said.

"Oh!" Laura said. "Is that true? Do you think that Gilbert hurt Farley? I hope that Farley is OK."

"I don't want to worry about that now," Ray said.

———

After about an hour, we stopped at a coffee shop beside a gas station. Laura gave me one of her dresses and I took off my wet clothes in the ladies' restroom. I was cold, but Laura's dry clothes warmed me as soon as I put them on.

When we were eating, I said, "We go through Little Rock, Arkansas on this road. We can stop at Little Rock airport. I'll call a friend and ask him to buy me a ticket to Santa Teresa." I turned to Ray. "When you get to Louisville, how are you going to find Johnny's hiding place for the money?"

"Maybe my mother knows something," said Ray. "Johnny said, 'If anything happens to me, I'll leave a message with your Ma.' He wanted me to come to California when I got out of jail. He wanted the two of us to go back to Louisville and collect the money. That was his plan. We need that big iron key to get into the hiding place, that's all I know."

"What key?" asked Laura.

Ray didn't answer her. "Do you still have it?" he asked me.

"I can get it," I said.

"Good," he said. "I don't want you to disappear with it."

"Do you think that I'm going to help you?" I said. "You're going to find the money, and take Chester's share too."

"Chester tried to take what was mine," Ray said. "He'll probably not pay you either."

"I don't want to think about that," I said.

10

Helen Rawson

After we finished eating, Ray got into the back of the car and fell asleep. I sat in the passenger seat and Laura drove.

"So you never had any time with Ray when you were younger?" I said to her.

"No," she said. "After Ray and my mother got divorced, she made me write to him once a month. Then she got married again and forgot about Ray."

"What about your stepfather?" I said. "What's his story?"

"Paul? He and Gilbert are real good friends," she said. "If Paul hears anything bad about Gilbert, he doesn't believe it. And my mother repeats whatever Paul says." She glanced at me. "Are you married?"

"I was," I said. "Twice."

"Gilbert was loving and kind to me at first," Laura said. "And being with him was great. But he doesn't trust people. Sometimes when he drinks alcohol, he cries like a baby. Then he makes me real sad—he breaks my heart."

"And your nose," I said.

Later, I drove the car and Laura sat beside me. Then she fell asleep, too.

When I stopped for gas outside the town of Texarkana, Laura got into the driver's seat again. We had now left the state of Texas and were in Arkansas. After a short time, I fell asleep.

When I woke up, I looked out of the car window and saw a highway sign that said U.S. 40. We were traveling north.

"How far is it to Little Rock?" I asked.

"We've passed Little Rock," said Laura.

"What?! I told you—"

"You had the map and you were asleep," she interrupted. "I don't know where Little Rock airport is. And there are no flights at one o'clock in the morning. I'm tired. It's time to find a motel."

We found a motel soon after this, and Ray woke up.

"Where are we?" he said.

"We're in Arkansas," I said. "But we've passed Little Rock. The next city is Memphis, Tennessee."

"I thought that you were leaving us at Little Rock."

"So did I," I said.

We booked two motel rooms, one for Laura and me, the other for Ray. We arranged to meet him at six o'clock in the morning.

———

We drove into the state of Tennessee and entered Memphis at seven o'clock the next morning. I sat in the back of the car and looked out of the window. I wanted to find a public phone and call Henry. Then I remembered that Santa Teresa time was two hours behind Memphis time. It was now 5 a.m. in Santa Teresa—too early to call him.

Laura saw me looking down the streets for a phone booth. "I know that you want to get home, but can't you come with us to Louisville?" she said.

"I want to go to Nashville airport," I said. "We'll be there by the middle of the morning. I can catch a flight to Santa Teresa from there."

"Come to Kentucky with us," Ray said to me. "We'll take you to my mother's house in Louisville. You can have a hot shower and a meal. You can put your clothes in Ma's washing machine. Later, we'll take you to Louisville airport and we'll pay for your ticket."

"We will?" Laura said. "Why?"

"Listen, Kinsey is only here because of us," Ray said. "And Chester is never going to pay her."

"You like giving people money that you don't have," Laura said to him.

He pointed at the money vest on her stomach. "Are you saying that I'm not getting any of that?"

"No, I'm not saying that," she replied. "But this trip is costing us a lot of money."

Ray turned to me. "Please will you come to Louisville?"

I hesitated for a moment. "OK," I said.

———

We reached Louisville just before midday. Laura stopped the car outside the house where Ray's mother lived. Helen Rawson's house had two narrow front windows and three steps up to the front door. There was another entrance at the side of the house, and Ray walked towards this with Laura and me behind him. All the windows had metal bars across them. Through one window I could see a light.

Ray knocked on the side door. Inside the house, another light was switched on. A hand pulled one of the drapes back

74

from the window and an elderly woman looked out. She was short, with a soft round face and round glasses. Her thinning hair was white and pulled up in a knot on the top of her head. Behind her round, thick glasses, the old woman's eyes were weak—she couldn't see well.

"What do you want?" she shouted through the glass.

Ray shouted back. "Ma, it's me, Ray."

Helen Rawson stared at her son for a few seconds, then she put her hands up to her mouth. A few minutes later, she unlocked the door.

"Ray!" she said, and threw herself into his arms.

Ray laughed, holding her close against his chest. Mrs Rawson was about half his size. She stepped away from him and looked at her granddaughter. "Who's this?" she asked.

"It's me, Grandma—Laura. How are you?" Laura replied. Then the young woman turned toward me. "And this is Kinsey Millhone. She came with us from Dallas."

"Laura, my dear!" The old lady's eyes were full of tears. "This is wonderful!"

Laura kissed her grandmother. Helen Rawson didn't say anything about Laura's "pregnant" stomach.

"Come inside, all of you," she said.

We stepped into a hallway of the house and waited for Mrs Rawson to lock the door behind us. To the right, there were some dark narrow stairs. To the left, there was a kitchen and Helen Rawson led the way into this room. The kitchen stove was very old, and there was a big table with four chairs in the center of the room. There was one window above the sink, and an old kitchen cabinet to the left of the door. Helen began to make some coffee.

Ray moved piles of newspapers from the chairs and he and I sat down. Laura said, "Excuse me," and went to a room at the back of the house. From my position, I could see part of the dining room. It was full of furniture and cardboard boxes.

Beyond the dining room there was a living room, with the two windows that looked out onto the street.

After some minutes, Laura returned to the kitchen. She was no longer wearing the money vest under her dress.

"How am I going to feed you all?" Ray's mother said. "I don't have enough food in the house."

"Write a list of the things that you need," Ray said. "We'll go to the market and buy everything. Kinsey has some clothes to put in your washing machine. Is that OK?"

"Yes, of course," his mother said.

"And I'd like to borrow your phone, and a pen and some paper, please," I said.

The phone and phone book were in the bedroom at the back of the house. I called American Airlines. There was a flight from Louisville to Chicago at 7:12 p.m. From Chicago, I could get a plane to Los Angeles which would arrive at 10:24 p.m., California time. The flight to Santa Teresa left at 11:30 p.m., arriving forty-five minutes later.

While I was waiting for the ticket agent to check all this information, Ray came into the bedroom with a clean towel.

"Use this when you shower," he said. "There's a bathrobe[87] that you can wear after your shower. It's behind the door. Ma will wash your clothes in the washing machine. There's a dry cleaner's[88] near the market. Give me your jacket. We'll leave it at the dry cleaner's before we start shopping and we'll collect it afterwards."

"OK." I took everything out of the pockets of my jacket and gave it to him.

Ray left the room and I finished the phone call to the airport. Then I went into the bathroom. After a quick search, I found Laura's money vest in a basket where dirty linen is kept before it's washed. The money was still in the vest. There were five-, ten-, twenty-, and fifty-dollar bills in the pockets of the vest. Most of them were very old, some were new. I put the vest back in the basket.

I gave Ray's mother my dirty, wet clothes and she put them in the washing machine. "Can I help with anything, Mrs Rawson?" I asked.

"No, dear," she said. "And please call me Helen. Go and have your shower. You can wear that bathrobe until your clothes are clean and dry."

After my shower, I phoned Henry. He was not at home, but I left a message on his answering machine[89]. "Henry, this is Kinsey," I said. "I'm in Louisville, Kentucky. It's after 1 p.m. here and I'm catching a plane at seven. Can you meet me at Santa Teresa airport? Please call me here." Then I repeated Helen's phone number.

Ray and Laura came back with the food and my cleaned jacket. Laura went to the bathroom for a shower while I helped Helen to prepare supper.

"Ma, do you have any mail for me?" Ray asked. "My friend in California was going to send me a letter."

"Yes," Helen said. "It came some time ago. It's in there." She pointed toward the drawer in the kitchen table.

Ray opened the drawer and pulled out a handful of envelopes. Only one was addressed to him and he opened it. He pulled out a folded card with a black-and-white photograph of a cemetery[90] stuck on the front. There was a thick line of black ink around the edge of the card. Inside the card there were some words from the Bible:

And I will give you the keys to heaven. Matthew 16:19.

Thinking of you at this sad time.

A small key was stuck to the back of the card. Ray pulled the key off the card and looked at it before he gave it to me. The word MASTER was on one side of the key and M550 was on the other.

"It's probably for a padlock," I said.

"What about the key that you've got?" Ray asked.

The word MASTER was on one side of the key and M550 was on the other.

"It's in the bedroom," I replied. "I'll get it when Laura's finished in there."

Supper was on the table when Laura came into the kitchen. I went into the bedroom and picked up my small knife from the table beside the bed. I cut open the lining of my jacket and took out the large iron key. It had the word LAWLESS on it, but there were no other markings.

I returned to the kitchen and gave the key to Ray.

"What's that for?" Laura asked.

"I'm not sure, but I think it has to be used with this one," Ray said and he put both keys in the middle of the table. "Johnny had the big one in his apartment, inside a safe. Chester found it."

"Are these keys connected to the hidden money?" Laura asked.

"I hope so," Ray said.

We ate our meal. I was hungry and I didn't listen carefully to the conversation between Ray and Laura until Ray said, "You called her? When?"

Laura's face became red. "I called my mother when we arrived here. I didn't want her to worry about me."

"Marla will tell Gilbert where you are," Ray said. "Believe me, Gilbert will make her tell him. When he started breaking my fingers, I couldn't wait to answer his questions. Did you warn your mother?"

"What about?" Laura said.

"What do you think? Gilbert's going to kill me," Ray said. "He's going to kill you, too. He'll kill Kinsey, your grandmother, and anybody else who tries to stop him. He wants the money. We've got to get out of here."

"What's happening, son?" Helen said. "I don't understand."

"Just get your coat, Ma," Ray said.

We began to move quickly. I got my clean clothes and put

them on in the bedroom. Then I put on my jacket, and started putting my things in the pockets.

Suddenly, Laura screamed in the kitchen and I heard a plate fall and break on the floor.

I pushed the last of my things into my pockets and ran into the kitchen. Helen, Ray and Laura weren't moving.

Gilbert was standing in the doorway of the dining room with a gun in his hand. He was pointing it at me.

11

Gilbert Hays

Gilbert stood in the doorway, smiling. "Marla couldn't come with me," he said. "She's not feeling very well."

When she heard her mother's name, Laura started to cry.

"Put up your hands," Gilbert told her.

Ray was wearing his jacket and had his car keys in his hand. Helen had her coat on. She stood by the table with her hands raised. We all had our hands up. It was almost funny.

I watched Gilbert. He had the gun in his right hand. He put his left hand into his jacket pocket and brought out a roll of adhesive tape.

"Ray, sit in that chair," he said, still smiling. "Laura is going to tie you with this tape. Stop crying, baby." He threw the roll of tape to Laura. "Everybody stay calm and quiet, or I'll shoot you. Grandma won't look very good with a bullet hole in her head. Neither will Ray look good with a big hole in his chest."

"Gilbert, please—" Laura began.

"*Tape him!*" Gilbert screamed.

Ray sat in a chair and Gilbert looked at me. "Give me the keys," he said.

I reached for the two keys on the table and put them in his left hand. He glanced at them, then put them in the pocket of his jacket.

Ray said, "Listen, Gilbert. You can do anything that you want to with me, but leave the others alone."

"I can do anything that I want to," Gilbert said. "And I'm going to do it. I don't care about the old woman, or *her*." He looked at me. Then he pointed at Laura. "But *she* ran away from me. Get on with the taping," he told her. "Tape his feet to the chair and tie his hands behind him."

"It's OK," Ray said to Laura. "Do it."

"Tie the tape tightly, or I'll blow a hole in his leg," said Gilbert.

"OK!" she said. She was angry now. "Where's Farley?"

Gilbert smiled. "I left him in California. He doesn't like to get hurt, so he told me everything." Gilbert walked across to Ray's chair and checked the tape. "After you finish with him, you can tape her." He pointed at me.

"What did you do to Farley?" Laura asked.

"*I* didn't do anything," Gilbert said. "*You* did. You ran away from me, baby. You never learn, do you?"

"Farley's...dead?" she said. She started to cry again.

"Yeah, he is," Gilbert said quietly. "How many times have I told you? You've got to do what I say. You didn't do what we planned. You didn't fly to Rio. And Farley? Well, I think that we've said enough about him."

Then Helen said, "Young man, I want to take my coat off and I want to sit down. I'm eighty-five years old and my legs and feet are painful."

"Sit down but don't touch anything," Gilbert said.

"Thank you." Helen took off her coat and sat down.

"Where's the money?" Gilbert asked Laura.

"In—in the bedroom," she said.

"Finish taping Ray and bring it here."

"We only have $8000," Laura said. "You talked about a million."

Gilbert didn't seem surprised. Farley had probably told him about the $8000 when he told Gilbert everything else.

Laura returned from the bedroom with the vest. Gilbert took it from her and looked at the money. "Where's the rest?" he asked Ray. "There was two million dollars' worth of money and valuables in that bank. Where are the jewelry, the coins, and the other things?"

"None of us knew exactly what was in that bank," Ray said. "None of us ever saw a million dollars. How much money was there? We don't really know because we never had a chance to count it."

"There was a lot more than this," Gilbert said. "We took seven or eight bags of money and valuables from that bank. So where did Johnny hide it all?"

"I don't know," Ray said. "He didn't tell me."

"Maybe he spent it," I said.

"Maybe," Ray said. "I know that he sent money to Ma."

Gilbert looked quickly at Helen. "Is that right?"

"Oh, yes," she said. "He sent me $500 every month since 1944. The money stopped arriving some months ago—in July or August."

"Five hundred a month?" Gilbert said. "That's crazy!"

"That's $246,000," Ray said. "And Johnny kept $500 a month for himself. After forty-one years, that makes a total of $492,000 dollars. If we took half a million from the bank. That leaves about $8000."

Gilbert moved across the room and put the gun against Ray's head. "*I know that there was more and I want it!*" he screamed. "Tell me the truth or I'll blow your head off!"

"Kill me and you'll never find the money," Ray said, calmly. "I knew Johnny well. I can think like him."

Gilbert moved the gun away from Ray's head. "All right, this is the plan. I'm taking Laura with me. Tomorrow, we'll go and get the money—or I'll kill her. OK?"

"No!" Ray said. "I need more time."

"You'll show me where the money is tomorrow," Gilbert said. "Or I'll kill Laura."

"Where will I find you?" Ray asked.

"*I'll* find *you*," Gilbert said.

Suddenly Helen said, "I've been sitting down too long. Can I stand up?"

"OK, old woman," said Gilbert. Then he laughed. "But don't try to run out of here for help."

"Don't worry about me," Helen said. "Worry about my friend, Freida Green."

"Who's she?" Gilbert asked.

"Freida Green is my neighbor," said Helen. "She lives with her friend, Minnie Paxton. About four months ago, burglars broke into houses in this street, and it frightened us. Afterwards, Minnie had a plan. We each made a shelf under a table in our houses and we keep a gun there—like this one."

Helen stood up and pulled a large gun from under the table.

The four of us stared at the old woman. Because she couldn't see very well, Helen was pointing the gun at the window and not at Gilbert.

"Drop that!" he said.

"Drop *your* gun," she replied.

I expected Gilbert to shoot her, but he said calmly, "That's a heavy gun. Your arms are going to get tired."

"I'll shoot you before that happens," Helen said.

"You're not strong enough to—" Gilbert didn't say anything more. He was interrupted by a bullet that went

Helen stood up and pulled a large gun from under the table.

past his right ear and through the kitchen window. Other bullets cut his ear and neck.

Laura screamed and threw herself down onto the floor, but I was down there before her. Ray pushed his chair over and lay on his side. Gilbert shouted with pain and dropped his gun.

"This time I'll blow *your* head off," Helen said loudly.

Gilbert grabbed Laura's hair. He pulled her up in front of him. With his other hand, he picked up the money vest.

"If you shoot at me again, I'll break her neck," he said.

He moved back into the dining room, pulling Laura with him. I heard the sound of breaking glass as he kicked the front door open. Then they were gone.

———

Helen's body was shaking with fear and her face was pale. She sat down in a chair. "Where did Gilbert go?" she asked. "What's happening?"

"He's got Laura, Ma," Ray said. "But everything's going to be OK."

I got a kitchen knife and cut the tape from his hands and feet. Soon he was free from the chair.

"I—I should have killed him," Helen said. Her body was shaking again.

Ray took his mother into the bedroom and helped her into her bed. I found Gilbert's gun and picked it up carefully with my knife. The police could check his fingerprints on the gun. They could use this information when Gilbert went to court for his crimes.

I put the gun on the kitchen table, then knocked softly on the bedroom door. Ray opened it a few inches.

"We must call the police," I said.

"Don't do that," he whispered.

"Why not?"

"I'll be out in a minute, as soon as Ma is asleep. You and I

85

need to talk." He shut the door again.

While I waited, I picked up the glass from the broken window. I heard Ray talking on the phone in the bedroom. Maybe he *was* calling the police. He came back into the kitchen, closing the bedroom door behind him. He saw Gilbert's gun on the table and picked it up. He pushed it into his belt.

"Now you've spoiled Gilbert's fingerprints," I told him.

"Nobody's going to check this gun for fingerprints," Ray said. He went into the dining room and came back with a piece of cardboard. He used some of Gilbert's adhesive tape to fix the cardboard across the broken window.

"I heard you talking on the phone," I said. "Did you call the police?"

"No. I called Marla," he said. "Gilbert beat her and broke her nose. But she doesn't want to go to the cops while he's got Laura."

"*You* could go to the police, Ray."

"Let's look for the money first."

"Why don't you want to go to the police?" I said. "What's the problem?"

He didn't answer. And then I started thinking.

"Did they *let* you out of prison, Ray, or did you *escape*?" I said suddenly.

"It wasn't really a jail," he replied. "We weren't locked in at night."

"But you weren't allowed to *leave*," I said. "You were still a prisoner. Right?"

He didn't answer.

"Prisoners don't have drivers' licenses. How did you get a driver's license?" I asked.

"I didn't. I don't have one."

"You've been driving without a driver's license? How did you rent a car without one?"

"I didn't," he replied.

"You *stole* the rental car?" I said.

"Yeah. So we can't go to the cops. If we find the money, Gilbert won't kill Laura."

I was angry now. "This isn't my problem," I said. "You don't want to call the police? OK. I'm leaving."

"Are you going back to California?"

"Yes," I said. "Two old friends of mine are getting married on Thanksgiving Day. That's in two days' time. I'm going to be a guest at their wedding. But now Gilbert has got the $8000 and you can't pay for my plane ticket. But you *can* drive me to the airport."

Then Ray got angry, too. "Laura is going to die, but do you care? No! You could have helped, but you said 'no.'" He softened his voice again and put his hand on mine. "I need your help," he said. "Help me to think. You've got hours until your flight leaves. We must find the rest of the money."

I had no plane ticket and couldn't pay for one. But maybe Henry could pay for my ticket on his credit card. When Helen woke up, I could phone him.

I stared at Ray. What was I going to do? Should I help him to get Laura back? Or should I get out of Louisville as fast as I could? I'd broken many laws during this case. I'd broken into hotel bedrooms. I'd helped criminals.

I sat down. Why didn't I walk out of the house, find a phone, and call Henry immediately? I don't know. I guess that I wanted to help this man and his family.

At that moment, Helen came out of the bedroom. "I feel better," she said. "What's happening? What are we going to do?"

"We must think where Johnny hid the money," Ray said. I went into the bedroom and phoned Henry, but he wasn't at home. I left another message on his answering machine, then I went back into the kitchen again.

87

"Let's start with the keys," I said. "Let's write down everything that we can remember about them."

Ray smiled. He got a pen and a piece of paper and wrote the word "keys" at the top of the paper.

"One key was a Lawless," I said. "It was old, it was made of iron, and it was about six inches long. The other was a Master…" I hesitated. Then I said, "Do you have a phone book?"

Ray got the book from the bedroom. There were no companies in the phone book called Lawless who made keys. But there was an address for an old company called the Louisville Locksmith Company.

"We'll try them," I said. "Maybe they know about old Lawless keys. And we'll also look in the old phone books in the public library."

I looked at our list again. "The other key was a Master. Master is a company that only makes padlocks. Could the hiding place have a big door and then a smaller door?"

"Maybe," Ray said. "Johnny would have chosen a place that was strong and safe. He needed a hiding place that no one would find. And he would have chosen a building that wouldn't be destroyed for a long time."

"Maybe the keys open doors in an old church," Helen said. "Or a school."

We were silent for a minute or two. Then I said, "Where in Louisville did the police catch Johnny?"

"I don't remember," Ray said. "He was caught somewhere outside the town."

"Ballardsville Road," Helen said. "I heard it on the radio news report. I was frightened because I thought that you were with him, Ray."

"How soon after the robbery did the police catch Johnny?" I asked.

"Half a day," Ray said. "And the things that we stole from

the bank were heavy. He had to move seven or eight heavy bags."

"So he didn't hide them very far away from the bank," I said. "The money is probably in Louisville. The little key had M550 on it. We could ask a locksmith to make us one like it."

"OK," Ray said. "Let's go."

"I'm not staying here on my own, Ray," Helen said. "I'm coming with you." She got her coat.

12

Lawless

The owner of the Louisville Locksmith Company was Whitey Reidel.

"Mr Reidel, we need an M550 Master padlock key," I told him.

"I can't help you," he said. "No Master padlock key starts with an M."

"I remember the numbers clearly," I said.

"Then somebody put them on the key after it was made," Mr Reidel said.

"Have you ever heard of a Lawless lock?" I asked.

"No, I've never heard the name. Maybe it's foreign."

"Was there a Lawless locksmith company in the 1940s?" I asked.

"No," he said.

"Are you *sure?*" I said.

Ray put his hand on my arm. "Let's go, Kinsey." Then he looked at Mr Reidel and said, "Thanks for your help."

It was now late afternoon. Outside, the sky was almost

dark. A cold wind was blowing and there was snow in the air. We drove back to Helen's house.

Had Henry called while we were out? I didn't know. Helen didn't have an answering machine.

———

We had supper, then Helen went into her bedroom to watch TV. Ray washed the dishes. I was putting them away in the kitchen cabinet when I noticed the card from Johnny. I picked it up and looked at it again.

Ray saw me looking at the card. "Read the message again," he said.

I opened the card and read the words aloud.

"*'And I will give you the keys to heaven. Matthew 16:19. Thinking of you at this sad time.'* Maybe M550 is a clue to another part of the Bible," I said. "Maybe M550 is Matthew chapter five, verse fifty."

"Chapter five of Matthew only has forty-eight verses," Ray said. He smiled at my surprised face. "When I was in prison, I read the Bible a lot."

I closed the card and looked at the black-and-white photo on the front. It was a picture of a cemetery that was covered in snow. All the gravestones were old. There were five small headstones and three large monuments. Some of the old monuments had tall iron railings around them.

The biggest monument was white and it had the name PELISSARO on it.

"Do you recognize this cemetery?" I asked Ray.

"No," he said. "Anyway, Johnny didn't have time to dig a hole and bury the money. We robbed the bank during the winter of 1944 and the ground was hard."

"It was winter?" I said. "Maybe this photograph was taken at that time. But why did Johnny send you a picture of a monument in a cemetery? And is the Pelissaro monument important? Maybe Johnny had a friend called Pelissaro."

I looked in the phone book, but there were no families called Pelissaro in it.

"Maybe there was a Pelissaro in the 1940s. We'll check the phone books in the library tomorrow." I opened the book at the page marked CEMETERIES. "Do you have a map of Louisville?"

Ray went out to the car and came back with a road map.

I showed him the names of cemeteries in the phone book. "Are any of these near the place where Johnny was caught?" I said. We went through the list. There were five cemeteries near to the place where Johnny was arrested.

"Tomorrow morning, we'll call each of these cemeteries," I said. "Maybe one will have a Pelissaro monument."

I slept upstairs in a small cold bedroom and woke early the next morning. When I got down to the kitchen, Ray was reading the newspaper and Helen was making breakfast. Gilbert's gun was lying on the table.

After I finished eating, I phoned each of the five cemeteries. Only one—the Twelve Fountains Cemetery—had a Pelissaro buried there. I told Ray.

"I hope that you're right about this," he said.

I went to have a shower. While I was washing my hair, I heard the phone ring. Ray answered it. When I got back to the kitchen, he was putting some tools on the table—some rope, a hammer, two shovels, a pickax and a hand drill[91].

"Gilbert phoned. He's coming here with Laura," he said. "I said that we might have some ideas where the money is hidden." He took Gilbert's gun from the table and pushed it into his belt.

Half an hour later, Gilbert and Laura arrived. They had the duffel bag with them, and Gilbert was wearing his Stetson again. There were injuries on his neck and ear where the bullets from Helen's gun had hit him. Laura looked very tired. She started to go toward her grandmother, but Gilbert stopped her. He put a hand on the back of Laura's neck and said something quietly into her ear. She said nothing.

Then Gilbert saw the gun in Ray's belt. "Give me that," he said.

"I want the keys first," Ray replied.

Suddenly, Gilbert's right hand went to Laura's neck, and I saw that he was holding a knife in his right hand. The knife made a small cut in Laura's skin and blood ran down her neck. "Daddy!" she cried.

Ray took the gun from his belt and gave it to Gilbert. "Here, take it," he said. "Move the knife away from her neck."

Gilbert moved the knife to his left hand and took the gun with his right. "We've got to trust each other," he said to Ray. "When I get my share of the money, she can go with you."

"OK," Ray said.

"He's not going to share the money with us," Laura said suddenly. She started to cry. "Tell him where it is before he kills me."

"I've waited forty years for this money!" Ray shouted. He was angry with her now. "I'm buying your life, Laura, but it isn't cheap. My business is with him, OK?"

Laura stopped crying. Gilbert was enjoying this argument.

I listened while Ray told him the plan. Ray didn't say the name of the cemetery, or the name on the monument.

"We haven't found the money yet, but we're getting close," he said. "Do you have the keys with you?"

Gilbert took them from his pocket, then he put them away again. "The old lady is coming with us," he said. "I don't trust her. She could call the cops."

"She won't do that," Ray said.

Gilbert put one hand around Laura's neck again. "We're all going together," he said.

92

The Twelve Fountains Cemetery was several miles from Louisville. There was a small office near the entrance, on the other side of some tall iron gates.

Ray drove the car through the gates and stopped the car outside the office. Gilbert took Helen with him into the building. Laura had bruises on her face, and he didn't want people to see these marks and ask questions.

After a few minutes, Ray and Helen came back to the car with two maps of the cemetery. The smaller map showed the part of the cemetery that we needed to visit. On the larger map, one area was marked with a red circle. Gilbert showed this map to Ray and pointed to the red circle.

"The Pelissaro monument is there," he said.

Ray drove through the cemetery until he found the Pelissaro monument. Then he parked the car and we all got out.

It was a cold winter's day and there were no other people near us in the cemetery. I looked at the monument in the photo on the card and then I looked at the monument in front of us. It was the same. The building was made of white stone and it was taller than all the headstones around it.

Gilbert threw his Stetson onto the back seat of the car. "What do we do now?" he asked Ray.

"Let me think for a minute," Ray said.

He looked at the headstones, the trees, and the hills in the distance. I did the same. We were both looking for some kind of clue. The Pelissaro monument had to be important. Ray was looking at the names on the gravestones. I slowly turned around in a circle. There were five mausoleums around us. Each small building in the circle was different, and a family's name was written above the door on each one. REDROX. HARTFORD. WILLIAMSON. And...LAWLESS.

I put a hand on Ray's arm and pointed at the fifth mausoleum. "There," I said.

"Give me the keys," Ray said to Gilbert.

We all went to the Lawless mausoleum. At the entrance, there was an old iron gate with a keyhole. Through the bars of the gate and around the main lock, there was a chain with a padlock. I looked at the smaller map of this part of the cemetery. The Lawless mausoleum was in the "M" section of the cemetery. It was on an area of ground with the number 550.

Ray walked to the car. It was parked in the circle opposite the Lawless mausoleum. "Come and get some tools," he told us, and we did. Then we watched him put the small key into the Master padlock. He turned the key and the lock opened. The chain fell through the bars of the gate and dropped onto the ground. The big, iron key opened the lock in the gate. Ray pushed the gate open and we walked in.

There were sixteen burial vaults. Twelve of these vaults had headstones, with names and dates on them. The others were covered with plain concrete and were nameless.

Ray and Gilbert used the pickax and a shovel. They started to break open the highest concrete-covered vault. Laura started work on the lowest, hitting it with the other shovel. Helen and I moved back to the wall and watched.

I checked the time on my watch—10:15 a.m. If I could catch an early flight, I would be home in time for supper. Tomorrow was the day before Rosie and William's wedding. Nell, Klotilde and I would eat at Rosie's restaurant tonight.

I thought about the wedding for a long time. The next thing that I knew, Ray, Gilbert and Laura were pulling canvas bags out of the building.

Helen and I watched Ray empty one of the bags onto the ground outside the mausoleum.

"Look at that!" Ray said. "That's beautiful!"

There were coins, stamps, jewelry, documents, American and foreign money, and gold and silver dollars.

There were coins, stamps, jewelry, documents, American and foreign money, and gold and silver dollars.

Just then, it started to rain.

"Let's go," Ray said.

Laura put everything back into the bag while Gilbert and Ray took the other bags out of the mausoleum and put them into the trunk of the car. As Ray put the last bag in the car, I looked across at Gilbert. He had taken his gun out of his pocket.

Gilbert looked at Ray and smiled. "Truth time," he said. "Johnny Lee paid me to kill Darrell McDermid."

"No!" Ray said. "Darrell died in an accident."

"It wasn't an accident," Gilbert said. "I killed him."

"Why? Did you murder him because he talked to the cops?" Ray asked.

Gilbert smiled again. "Johnny said that Darrell told the cops about the robbery. He believed that. But Johnny was wrong. I told the cops."

"You were never a nice guy, Gilbert," Ray said. He put his hand behind his back. When I saw Ray's hand again, he was holding a gun.

Gilbert laughed. "This will be fun," he said. "Who dies first?"

"This will be more fun for me than for you," Ray said.

"Daddy, don't—" said Laura.

"You don't have to do this, Ray," I said, "There's plenty of money—"

"This isn't about money," Ray said. "This is about a guy who's been beating Marla and my daughter. It's about a guy who murdered Darrell and Farley."

I was busy watching the two men and I wasn't watching Helen. Suddenly, she threw a shovel at Gilbert. The shovel missed Gilbert, but it hit Ray on the arm.

"Ma!" Ray shouted.

I saw Gilbert point his gun at Helen. Then there was a CLICK! "What—?" he began.

Ray laughed. "Oh, I'm sorry. I forgot to tell you," he said. "You can't shoot me. I removed part of your gun last night." Then he lifted his own gun and shot Gilbert.

Gilbert fell to the ground and then Ray fired his gun again—twice. I watched, shocked. I couldn't move.

Ray turned and looked past me. "Don't do that!" he shouted. I half-turned—and saw Laura lifting a shovel above my head. Then she hit me.

———

I woke up in a bed in a hospital. I had the worst headache of my life and a huge bruise on my head.

Two police detectives asked me questions for several hours. They listened to my story, but I could see that they didn't believe a word of it. At last, the detectives phoned the offices of the Louisville newspaper and checked the story of the bank robbery in 1941. The news reports gave the names of the robbers and the story of the missing money.

The money and the rest of the valuables had disappeared. And Ray Rawson, his mother, and his daughter, Laura, were also missing. Gilbert Hays was dead.

I don't think that the police will ever find Ray and his family. They're now very rich. And I'm sure that Ray, Helen and Laura have used false names and gotten false passports. They are probably living in another country.

———

On Wednesday morning, I got out of the hospital.

I still hadn't had a call from Henry and I had no money. So at last, I called a friend who bought me a plane ticket and I caught a flight to Santa Teresa.

Rosie and William were married on Thanksgiving Day. William held his hands around Rosie's face and kissed her.

"Oh, my love," he said. "I've been waiting all my life for you."

Everybody cried, including me.

97

Points for Understanding

1

1 Henry asks Kinsey to do a favor. (a) When does he ask? (b) Who is the favor for? (c) What is it?
2 What does Kinsey learn about Johnny Lee from his grandson?
3 Who has come from Ashland to the apartment? Why has he come?

2

Why does Chester Lee believe that his father was hiding from the FBI?

3

1 What have the Lees found in Johnny's apartment?
2 Kinsey says, "Maybe Johnny never served in the Air Force." Then she makes a guess. (a) What is the guess? (b) Who is she talking to? (c) What does the person say?

4

1 Who is Kinsey following on the freeway? Why?
2 How does Kinsey find out the name of the woman in Row 8?
3 What surprising and interesting information does Kinsey think about on the hotel bus?

5

Kinsey pretends to be three different people on Saturday, November 23rd. Who does she pretend to be? Why?

6

1 Three keys are mentioned in this chapter. Who has them? What do they unlock?
2 What does Ray Rawson tell Kinsey about: (a) Johnny Lee? (b) himself? (c) Gilbert Hays?

7

1 How does Kinsey get the duffel bag from Laura's hotel room?
2 What is unusual about the five-dollar bill?

8

1 What does Kinsey now know about Laura?
2 What are the differences between the stories that Ray and Laura tell about the robbery?
3 Why was Johnny released from jail after two years?
4 Who is Farley? How is he connected to Laura?

9

1 Why does Kinsey want to get back to the Desert Castle hotel quickly? How does she get there?
2 What important thing has Kinsey left on the catwalk? Why is it there?

10

What has been mailed to Ray at Helen Rawson's house?

11

1 Why do you think that Ray puts Gilbert's gun into his belt?
2 Why must Kinsey get back to Santa Teresa by November 28th?
3 Where are Ray, Kinsey and Helen going? Why?

12

1 What is "Lawless"?
2 How do Ray, Gilbert, Kinsey, Laura and Helen find "Lawless" in the Twelve Fountains Cemetery?
3 Where do Gilbert and Ray use the pickax and a shovel? Why do they choose these places?
3 What truth does Gilbert tell the others about the robbery?
4 What happens to Kinsey? How does she get back to Santa Teresa?

Glossary

This book is written in American English. Compare:

AMERICAN ENGLISH	BRITISH ENGLISH
ahead	in front of
apartment	flat
bathrobe	dressing gown
dollar bill	banknote
center	centre
check	cheque
clerk	assistant
closet	cupboard
coffee shop	café
drapes	curtains
elevator	lift
favor	favour
flashlight	torch
freeway	motorway
gas	petrol
guy	man
highway	road
mail slot	letter box
Ma	Mum
parking lot	car park
restroom	toilet
trunk	boot
vacation	holiday
yard	garden

1 **burglar** (page 4)
   a person who goes into a building and steals something is called a
   burglar. The burglar is *breaking into* that place. The crime is called
   a *break-in*, or a *burglary.*
2 **favor** (page 7)
   if you help a person, and you don't expect payment, you are doing
   that person a *favor*.

3 **hesitate**—*to hesitate* (page 7)

wait before you do or say something because you are afraid, or nervous, or thinking carefully.

4 **divorced**—*to be divorced* (page 7)

if two people do not have a happy marriage and they do not love each other any longer, they can end their marriage. They get *divorced*.

5 **landlord** (page 7)

a person who owns a room, a house, or an apartment that other people live in.

6 **Thanksgiving** (page 7)

a special holiday in the U.S. *Thanksgiving Day* is on the fourth Thursday in November. Families eat a special meal and think about all the things that they are grateful for.

7 **fighter pilot** (page 8)

a person who flies airplanes for the air force of their country and fights their country's enemies.

8 **Burma** (page 8)

the old name for the country in Southeast Asia that is now called Myanmar. The capital city is Rangoon.

9 **cremated**—*to be cremated* (page 8)

when a person dies, a ceremony called a *funeral* takes place. After the funeral, the body is either put into a hole in the ground—it is *buried*, or it is burnt in a fire—it is *cremated*. A *military burial* is when the person is buried by officials from the army, air force or navy.

10 **filled out**—*to fill out* (page 8)

write down information on papers, documents, or forms.

11 **Veterans Administration Office** (page 9)

a department of the U.S. government that helped Americans who fought for their country. When they left the air force, navy or army, the VAO paid these *veterans* some money each month. It also gave the veterans advice.

12 **personnel files** (page 9)

the U.S. government keeps information about each person who was in the army, navy or air force. These *personnel files* have details about those people's health and their education. The files also say where and when they fought.

13 **determined**—*to be determined* (page 9)

not allow anything or anyone to stop you doing something.

14 **hallway** (page 10)

a short corridor inside a building with doors along it. The doors lead into other rooms.

15 **death certificate** (page 10)

a paper that gives information about when and why a person died. A *birth certificate* is a paper that gives information about a person's date of birth, place of birth, and the names of that person's parents and grandparents.

16 **social security card** (page 10)

the U.S. government gives each working person a special number—a *social security number*—which is written on a *social security card*. People need this number to get money from the government if they lose their jobs, or if they are too old or ill to work. Each month, the government pays these people with a *social security check*—a piece of paper that can be exchanged for money.

17 **number or unit** (page 10)

each person who joins the army, air force or navy (the *military forces*) is given a *number*. A *unit* is a group of people who fight together.

18 **serve**—*to serve* (page 10)

people who join the military forces and fight for their country are *serving* their country. The time that the *servicemen* and *servicewomen* are in that force is called their *service*.

19 **military pension** (page 10)

an amount of money that veterans are paid by the government each month, after they leave their military force.

20 **rent**—*to rent* (page 11)

when you pay people so that you can live in their apartments or their houses, you are *renting* their properties from them. The amount of money you agree to pay every month, or every week, is the *rent*. The people who own the properties are *renting out* their properties.

21 **pretend**—*to pretend* (page 12)

behave or speak in a way that makes people believe that something is true, although it is not.

22 **checked**—*to check* (page 12)

look carefully at something.

23 **closet** (page 12)

a piece of furniture where clothes are kept.

103

24 **bills** (page 12)

a list showing the things that you've paid for in a restaurant, store, etc.

25 **thinning** (page 12)

if someone's hair has started to fall out, it is *thinning*.

26 **mail slot** (page 14)

mail (letters, parcels, etc.) is delivered by the post office. Letters and parcels are *mailed* by one person to another. Post office workers deliver the mail to people's houses by pushing it through the *mail slots*—wide, thin holes in their front doors.

27 **real** (adv.) (page 15)

very. Real mess = very untidy. Real good = very good.

28 **crime scene** (page 18)

the place where a crime happened. Police detectives study a crime scene to find clues about the crime. Every person has lines on the skin at the ends of his or her fingers. Whenever you touch something, the lines on your fingers leave marks. These marks are called *fingerprints*. Each person's fingerprints are different. When police officers investigate a crime scene, they study the fingerprints that they find there. The police may have notes about the criminal's fingerprints in their files.

29 **glanced**—*to glance* (page 18)

look quickly at someone or something.

30 **retire**—*to retire* (page 18)

when you become old and cannot work any longer, you *retire* from your work.

31 **connect**—*to be connected to* (page 19)

someone who has the same ideas or things as someone else, or goes to the same places, or does the same things as that other person, is *connected to* these ideas, things, places or events. Kinsey believes that there might be a *connection* between the break-in at the apartment and what Johnny Lee did in the war.

32 **FBI** (page 19)

a special police department in the U.S. that investigates important crimes and criminals for the whole country. The FBI headquarters are in Washington D.C., the capital of the U.S.

33 **Pentagon** (page 20)

the U.S. Department of Defense is the part of the government that is in charge of all the military forces. The main offices of the Department of Defense are in a large building in Arlington, Virginia. The building has five sides, so it is called the *Pentagon*.

104

34 **double agent** (page 20)

someone who is paid by a government to get secret information is a *spy*, or a *secret agent*. *Double agents* give their governments information about its enemies, but they also give their enemies information about their governments.

35 **panel** (page 22)

a flat, square piece of wood or metal that covers a secret space, or a hiding place.

36 **safe** (page 22)

a strong box made of thick metal where valuable things are kept. Safes may have two different kinds of locks. One kind of lock can only be opened with a special key. The other kind of lock—a *combination lock*—has numbers on it and you can only open this lock if you know the secret numbers.

37 locksmith (page 23)

a person who works with locks and keys. A *locksmith* can open many different locks using special tools. Locksmiths also make locks and keys. A *padlock* is used to join two things together, e.g. a gate. A padlock has a strong piece of metal across the top, which is opened with a key.

38 **adhesive tape** (page 23)

long, narrow, strong cloth that is sticky on one side. It is kept around a *roll*—a narrow ring of cardboard. *Adhesive tape* is used to join things together.

39 **prove**—*to prove* (page 26)

find something that shows that what you said or thought is true. The clues at a crime scene may be the *proof* that shows how the criminal committed the crime.

40 **lobby** (page 26)

an area inside the entrance of a building.

41 **operator** (page 27)

the person who helps to make phone calls to and from the guests in the hotel. The operator *connects* the phone lines between guests in two different rooms so that they can speak to each other.

42 **duffel bag** (page 30)

a large bag made from strong cloth with circular shapes at each end. It has many small pockets or compartments on the outside.

43 **Stetson** (page 30)

a hat named after John B. Stetson (1830-1906). *Stetsons* are worn by people in the western states of America. The hats are tall and they have broad brims.

44 license plate number (page 30)

every car has to be given permission—be *licensed*—by the government before anyone can drive it on a road. And each car has a different license number. The *license plate number* is shown on a piece of metal attached to the car.

45 PENNY-CAR-RENTAL (page 30)

if you do not own a car, or if you don't have your car during a journey, you can rent a car. You pay a *rental company* to use one of its cars.

46 motel (page 31)

a hotel close to a highway. The rooms of a *motel* are often separate small buildings, or cottages. Guests can usually park their cars next to their motel rooms.

47 carport (page 31)

a place beside a house where a car can be parked. A *carport* has a roof but no walls.

48 trunk (page 31)

the compartment at the back of a car where large things can be carried.

49 freeway (page 31)

a large, wide road. Travelers on *freeways* do not have to pay to use them. Travelers leave freeways by using *exits*—smaller, shorter roads.

50 parking lot (page 31)

a place where cars can be parked.

51 parking ticket (page 31)

in some parking lots you have to pay to leave your car there. Then you must put money into a machine and buy a *parking ticket* for the number of hours that you want to leave your car.

52 airport terminal (page 31)

the main building at an airport.

53 public phone booths (page 32)

tall boxes where anyone can go to make a phone call. *Public phone booths* are found on streets and in stores, hotels, restaurants, railroad stations and airports. *Phone books* contain lists of addresses and phone numbers for the people and companies in a town or city.

54 ticket counter (page 32)

the place in an airport where you can buy airplane tickets.

55 conveyor belt (page 32)

a moving path that carries your luggage out to an airplane.

56 **ticket agent** (page 32)

a person who sells airplane tickets.

57 **pregnant** (page 32)

a woman who is going to have a baby.

58 **credit card** (page 34)

a plastic card that is used instead of money. You have to repay the amount of money that you spend using your card, plus some extra, to the company who owns the card. Your *credit* is the amount of money that the card company will allow you to spend in one month.

59 **boarding pass** (page 35)

a document that shows where a passenger must sit during a plane flight.

60 **row** (page 35)

a line of seats. Rows of seats are usually given a letter or a number. Kinsey is sitting in the tenth row.

61 **luggage compartment** (page 35)

the place inside an airplane where you put your coat and hand luggage.

62 **passport** (page 35)

a small book that you get from your government. It contains your photograph and information about you. You have to show your *passport* at airports or borders, before you are allowed into other countries. *False* is something which is not true or real. A *false passport* contains incorrect information.

63 **phone charge card** (page 35)

a plastic card which can be used to pay for a number of phone calls.

64 **check in**—*to check in* (page 38)

when you arrive at a hotel to begin your stay, you give your details to the clerk at the reception desk. You *check in*. When you leave the hotel, you pay your bill and *check out*.

65 **cactuses** (page 39)

plants that grow in hot, very dry places. *Cactuses* have thick stems and sharp points instead of leaves.

66 **sewing kit** (page 39)

hotels often give their guests a small container—a *sewing kit*— which has needles, cotton thread and a pair of scissors inside it. You can use these things to *sew*, or join together the edges of a hole in your clothes.

107

67 **sales manager** (page 40)

a person who is in charge of selling goods and services.

68 **security** (page 40)

the way that people, buildings and property are kept safe. *Security cameras* are attached to the walls of buildings. The cameras film everyone who goes past them.

69 **Ms** (page 41)

Mr, Mrs, Miss and Ms are the titles that you use in front of a person's name if you are talking politely to them, or about them. Mr is used for a man, whether he is married or not. Ms is used for a woman, whether she is married or not. Miss is used for a woman who is not married. Mrs is used for a woman who is married.

70 **fire stairs** (page 41)

stairs in a building that people use if there is a fire and they cannot use the elevators. The stairs are made of metal or concrete and will not burn easily.

71 **linen carts** (page 42)

clothes, sheets, towels etc. are called *linen*. Hotels wash and dry large amounts of linen each day. Hotel staff take the linen to and from the rooms in *carts*. Carts are containers on wheels.

72 **bruises** (page 44)

dark marks that appear on a person's skin where they have been hit by someone or something.

73 **warn**—*to warn someone* (page 46)

if you tell someone that they are in danger, or that they must not do something, you are *warning* them not to do that thing. Your words are a *warning* and the person has been *warned*.

74 **lining** (page 47)

the piece of thin cloth that is attached to the inside of a jacket.

75 **eardrums** (page 48)

the skin inside your ears that helps you to hear sounds.

76 **grabbed**—*to grab* (page 53)

pick up something quickly.

77 **ladies' restroom** (page 54)

female toilets.

78 **five-dollar bill** (page 54)

a banknote that has a value of five dollars.

79 **cop** (page 56)

an informal word meaning "police officer."

80 **suspiciously** (page 56)

if you think that someone has done something wrong, but you are not sure, you are *suspicious* of that person. You *suspect* that person of something.

If you think that a thing or a person is strange, you might look at it or them *suspiciously*. And if something seems strange to you, and you are worried about it, that thing can be described as *suspicious*. But if you say, "He is *suspicious*," you mean that "He suspects somebody or something," not "I suspect him."

NOTE: the verb is pronounced su**pect**, the adverb is pronounced su**piciously** and the noun is pronounced **sus**pect.

81 **baby** (page 57)

an informal name that a man or woman uses for a person who he or she loves.

82 **bank's alarm** (page 60)

alarms are signals that tell people that they are in danger. Some alarms are have brightly flashing lights. Some alarms make a loud noise.

Bank alarms tell the police that someone has broken into the bank and is stealing something. *Fire alarms* tell the people in a building that there is a fire.

83 **statute of limitations** (page 64)

the length of time that passes between a crime taking place and when the police arrest the criminal is called the *statute of limitations*. For some crimes, if the police cannot solve the crime for a long time, the statute of limitations for that crime ends. Then the criminal might never go to jail for that crime.

84 **catwalk** (page 68)

a flat, narrow path of metal that is usually found high inside a building, near the roof. People use *catwalks* to work on roofs or high parts of buildings.

85 **water sprinklers** (page 68)

pipes that are fixed to the ceiling in a building. *Water sprinklers* throw water over the rooms if there is a fire.

86 **fire engines** (page 70)

large trucks that bring firefighters to a building where there is a fire. *Fire engines* carry water and the special equipment that firefighters use.

87 **bathrobe** (page 76)

a long, loose coat with a belt that is worn over nightclothes.

88 **dry cleaner's** (page 76)

a store where you take your clothes to be *dry-cleaned*. Chemicals, not soap and water, are used to clean the clothes.

89 **answering machine** (page 77)

a machine that records your phone messages for you while you are away.

90 **cemetery** (page 77)

an area of land where people are buried in graves when they die. A *headstone* is a flat piece of stone that is put over a dead person's grave. Words on the stone show the person's name and the dates of that person's birth and death. *Monuments* are large pieces of carved stone that are put on top of graves. *Mausoleums* are stone buildings in cemeteries that have dead people buried inside them. *Burial vaults* are compartments inside mausoleums where the bodies of dead people are placed.

91 **shovels, a pickax and a hand drill** (page 91)

shovels are tools that are used for digging in the ground and removing earth. A *pickax* is a tool with a long handle and a heavy metal spike at one end. It is used to make holes in hard ground. A *hand drill* is a machine that makes holes in wood, stone and metal.

Published by Macmillan Heinemann ELT
Between Towns Road, Oxford OX4 3PP
Macmillan Heinemann ELT is an imprint of
Macmillan Publishers Limited
Companies and representatives throughout the world
Heinemann is a registered trademark of Harcourt Education, used under licence.

ISBN 1–405–05778–5
EAN 978–1–405057–78–3

This retold version by John Escott for Macmillan Readers
First published by Macmillan 2005
Text © Macmillan Publishers Limited 2005
Design and illustration © Macmillan Publishers Limited 2005

This version first published 2005

Illustrated by Ruth Palmer
Cover image by Getty Images

Printed in Thailand

2009 2008 2007 2006 2005
10 9 8 7 6 5 4 3 2